The Side Effects of Love

L.C. AMOS

"Promote your potential and change the world"
Stay encouraged!

The Side Effects of Love is a work of fiction. Names, characters, places and incidents are products of the author's imagination or are used fictitiously. Any resemblance to actual events or locales or persons, living or dead, is entirely coincidental.

ISBN-10: 1499546319
ISBN-13: 978-1499546316

This book was printed in the United States of America.

Cover design by: L.C. Amos and Kylie Wilson
Cover photo by: Terrence Williams

DEDICATION

I dedicate this collection of words to
the loving memory of my aunt,
Denise E. "Peanut" Williams.
May you find comfort in the
arms of an angel…honey-honey!

February 14, 1966 – January 3, 2014

Chapter 1 - Nevaeh

With my head tilted slightly to the right, I ran my hands over my smooth, cocoa butter laced skin, allowing my hands to marvel at my curves. The way my body teased me as I stared at my womanly figure in the mirror made me shamefully feel a little bi- -- towards myself that is. I admired my facial features, pre-Mac make-up, separated my eyes, and spread my lips to check my teeth. Often times I had been mistaken for the actress LisaRaye McCoy and I could have passed for an acting stand in had it not been for my love of color. I would have been an unmistakable match.

I glided my paddle brush through my long, flowing tresses stopping every other stroke to examine my ends thinking once Dayna and I came back from our outing I would call Chanel to schedule a much needed hair appointment.

Just then, Jill Scott's *Hate on Me* came blasting through the speakers so I sashayed to my left and right and continued grooming.

The way some people approached me inquiring the brand and style of hair on my head – especially females – invoked a hideous chuckle inside. Most of them wanted to know whether or not I was rocking a full or partial sew-in on down to what color number was I wearing – was it a 1 or a 1-B. I hated to be the bearer of bad news but 'genetics' was often my answer.

Today was the day I had set aside to play hooky from a number of different projects. Normally, around this time of the year, business was booming with clients along the eastern seaboard that were anxious to learn the next greatest technique for student retention, more specifically black male retention as this population proved to be the most challenging. But, I had made plans to spend time with Dayna months ago. It seems like we had to sync our schedules just to spend time with one another. Our schedules kept us up to our neck with traveling and making business deals. Now that the holidays were coming soon, we both knew that it would be next to impossible to connect and enjoy some sisterly bonding.

My oldest sister, Dayna, was one of the baddest bakers in the Queen City. After college, she relocated to the Del-Mar-Va where she worked as an actuary. Boldly, she had given up a six-figure career to follow her dreams of opening her own bakery. Many people thought she was crazy, including that all-about-me sister of ours, Synatra, but in the end we were all glad that she followed her heart and stepped out on a leap of faith.

If there was one thing most entrepreneurs knew was that one of the best forms of advertising was word of mouth. We all knew that once the general public had gotten a sample of her baked goodies that they would come back clamoring for me. And that's just what set her business ablaze. Someone that knew Braylon, her powerful attorney and husband, recommended her to a couple of event promoters to provide a spread of confectionary delights for a CIAA day party a few years back. And the rest – as they say – is history.

Little did she know that the party would be attended by Gem, one of Braylon's clients. After they engaged in a brief conversation about the heights she planned to reach with her business, he introduced her to his wife, Anaise, who just happened to be a production assistant for an African-American female that was a multi-million dollar media mogul. Once she heard the name Harpo she immediately knew she was on to something special. In support of her vision, Gem offered to fly her and her team to Chicago for a feature spot on the Oprah Show, having her Key Lime Crème Cupcake added to one of Oprah's top 10 dessert list. And that was the shot heard around the world. Because of the almighty Oprah effect, her business spread like a California wildfire and she has never looked back.

She partnered with her husband, Braylon, to serve as her legal counsel and Jessica, her longtime assistant and friend, to serve as her event manager. Sometimes I sit back and look at my sister and admire her for her courage and perseverance. As she had shared with me many times, she would have never thought that she would be in business for fifteen years, but she was. The one thing that she was certain of was that she would always follow her heart, no matter what, with Braylon walking right by her side.

Reaching to change the track on my iPad, I grooved my way into the closet to find the perfect sister-girl outfit. I knew Dayna was already ready and probably on her way over. Sometimes, I thought to myself, married women could not possibly understand the troubles that single women often faced.

Dayna didn't have to worry about looking right for anyone but her husband. But, me, on the other hand, I had to put in a little extra effort to at least get a head-nod. Seems like lately the only interest I was getting was from married men, which did nothing to lessen my anxiety about marriage. If the only men that approached me were married, what did that say about the vibes I was putting off? I was not one for sharing a man and I was definitely no man's secret, but yet and still, I was single.

Finally able to put together a look, I held up the cream-colored blouse against my red shark-bite cardigan and admired the way they looked against the tan-colored linen pants that were laying at the foot of the bed.

"Ooh, that's my song," I sang as I danced the iron down the right leg and back up the left side. Just as Evelyn "Champagne" King was saying "Encore" I flipped my neatly folded pants over and gave the other side an encore of its own.

The time on the clock warned me that I had about thirty more minutes before Dayna would be impatiently ringing the doorbell. She hated to wait on people, especially me.

Once inside the warmed bathroom I started the water and situated my body care products along the edge of the shower wall. I tested a few drops on the inside of my wrist before immersing my tired and tensed up body under the massaging waterfall. A shower had always been my sanctuary. This is where I did some of my deepest thinking. Sometimes I thought about a variety of projects from the office or plans that I would attempt to make for the weekend that were most of the time overtaken by other competing priorities of a work nature. But most of all, this was where I came to pray and commune with the most high.

No sooner than I begun to bathe I heard the doorbell ring. And ring. And ring. It was definitely Dayna. I juggled my girls as I did a slight James Brown step after losing my balance. I quickly grabbed my robe from the back of the bathroom door and hurried over to the intercom on the wall nearest the entryway, leaving soapy size eight footprints along the way.

"I'm coming down right now. Give me a sec," I yelled before allowing Dayna the opportunity to vent her frustrations.

"I knew you were gonna be late. Hurry it up, chick!" Dayna said venting her frustrations anyway.

"Come on in." The door lock clicked twice and Dayna walked inside.

I could tell by the clinking sound that she had placed her keys in the oblong dish that donned the top of the side table in the foyer as she always did. I yelled down the steps as she yelled up the steps while pouring herself a glass of orange juice.

"Vay, sugah, what are you doing?" Dayna yelled in between sips. "You do know that time waits for no one, right and that includes me, too!"

"Girl, I'm coming. Keep your panties on!" I yelled from the top of the stairs. It's a good thing Dayna wasn't standing at the bottom of the staircase because she would have more than likely gotten a visual that was more than her eyes could handle.

I put the finishing touches on my outfit by looping a leopard print skinny belt around my waist to match my leopard print stilettos. I bounced my hair and my booty one last time and grabbed my keys and headed downstairs.

"Took you long enough, dang!" Dayna teased.

"There you go with all that time mess." I retorted, pausing next to the alarm site while Dayna made her way towards the front door. "So, what's the big rush anyway? We're just going to our usual spot, right?" After pressing the six-digit code for the alarm, I motioned for Dayna to open the door and we both walked out. At this time of day there would likely be a small wait at Miss G's Chicken and Waffles, affectionately named in honor of our late grandmother, but I also thought about the extra time we would have just to talk and catch up.

"Yeah. You know that's our spot."

Our baby sister Synatra had outdone herself. For someone who was a tender twenty-two and steadfast on opening the first mobile nail salon, she surprised us all by putting her cooking skills to use and opening up a restaurant instead. None of us really believed she had what it took to run her own business, mainly because she was just ghetto as hell and didn't have a clue about business or being professional. But, that girl was always full of surprises. She never stayed still long enough to finish a steady stream of pee, let alone meet a challenge like opening a restaurant head on. Although it took her four long years and three failed loan applications, she hung in there through all of the discouragement and disappointments. Once we finally knew that she was sure enough serious, we pitched in to help where we could and helped her to open the first chicken and waffles joint in Charlotte. No one had ever thought of the concept before either. Her blinged out establishment – with a taste of class – paid homage to all things tre'fo', our hometown better known as Winston-Salem. This included naming her most popular dish after the Mayor himself, appropriately named, The Mayor. The Mayor was the platter of all platters. It boasted a plate-sized flavored waffle, with three sides and three double-dipped, buttermilk fried chicken wings. It was a local favorite and we all were definitely a fan. It was enough food to feed a family of four with leftovers for lunch. And as much as she believed in giving people larger than life portions, you couldn't tell by the tiny frame she had.

She had items on the menu like "Who-Made-The-Potato Salad", "Boston Baked Beans" – coined after the housing project we all grew up in – and her world famous "Rev. Dr. Sterling Mack and Cheese" that she named after our family pastor. She couldn't keep enough of that in the kitchen. Some people would order it by the pan, thus prompting her to begin a soft catering venture on the side.

Just as I had suspected, there was a line winding out of the door and down the sidewalk. From the looks of things, the business lunch crowd had beaten us to the punch.

"I know one thing - the twelve o'clock lunch crew needs to hurry and high tail it on back to the office." Dayna had a thing about time and punctuality and her impatience was beginning to rear its ugly horns.

"Calm down. It'll be alright." I looked around to make sure no one was witnessing her untaught manners. "Besides, what you got planned after this anyway?"

"It's a surprise."

"Oh, no. I can't do *your* surprises. The last time you said 'it's a surprise' you ended up taking me to a strip club and you embarrassed the hell out of me."

I had just secured a major contract that Friday so Dayna told me that she was taking me out to celebrate. In going along with her surprise, she had the nerve to blind fold me, telling me that we were going on a treasure hunt. A pleasure hunt was more like it. After asking over and over again what was with all the noise, she finally removed the scarf from my face. I would have rather she have kept it on because when I finally regained my sight after struggling to reclaim my vision, the first thing I saw was a big, round gluteus that was maximized to the tenth power.

Some dancer dressed in a fuscia pink leather pant set had the open seated end of her anatomy smack dab against some guy's cheek...the one on his face. He seemed to enjoy the attention because instead of reaching for a Lysol wipe to cleanse the booty-dew from his face, he just wiped it with his hand and smelled it. Talk about disgusting. When I asked her what we were doing there, all she said was 'we are here to see the show like everyone else'. But, I knew better than that. She had made arrangements to have Braylon and one of his colleagues to meet us there in an attempt to play matchmaker. And Braylon, being who he is, agreed to go along with it. I loved my brother-in-law to death, but sometimes I just wanted to kill him for agreeing to all the foolishness that Dayna had sometimes put him up to. Once she saw that her rationale for having us there wasn't working as well as she'd planned, she made one more attempt at hooking me up with someone by telling me to pick any one of the men that was there. 'Girl, relax. This is where all the men hung out!' she told me. I passed. I figured if they were all in here then there must be a reason why they weren't at home with their wives, girlfriends, or significant others. No one in her right mind would want a man that hung out at the strip club all night long, spending all the bill money, and fantasizing about other women while he was with them. At least no man I would ever want.

"Well, this surprise is different."

"No, it's not. Not if it's at the hands of Dayna Yvonne Jones-Walters it's not."

"Sis, look at me. Look at my face" She pointed at her face as she displayed a not-so-good poker face. "Would I do you like that?"

"You *have* done me like that!" We both laughed. "No, seriously, where are we going?"

"I'll tell you more about it during lunch. Until then, you just have to wait." She retrieved her cell phone from her pocket and began to tap on the screen.

Another five minutes went by before our measly old party of two was called.

"Walters?" the short, stocky hostess called out.

"Right here", Dayna responded, as she held her hand up.

After updating the house layout, the young diva excitedly said, "Hey! Y'all are the owner's sisters, right?"

The expression on my face transformed from pleasant to puzzled in a matter of seconds.

"Why, yes we are," Dayna obliged, clearly feeling herself as having been identified as the *owner's* sister.

"I thought so. By the way, my name is Taryn and I am your hostess. I've only been here for a few weeks, but I make it a habit to learn about all of our customers, especially family," she air-quoted. She reached for another set of wrapped silverware and instructed us to follow her. "This way, please." Dayna mimicked her walk pretending to lead a party of two to our table.

We were seated in one of the half-moon booths near the private dining room where we began to look over the menu. It's not like we didn't know what to choose. We helped design the menu.

Once Taryn made sure we were seated comfortably, she began to tell us about the day's specials. To our delight, Taryn seemed very well versed on the restaurant operations for having only worked there a few weeks. I was sure to make a mental note to mention my observations to Synatra at our next business meeting.

Just then, a tall, thin gentlemen approached our table.

"Hello, lovelies. My name is Jermaine and I will be taking care of you today. May I start you ladies out with one of our delectable appetizers?"

Dayna continued to look at the menu. So I responded. "No, thank you, but we would like to go ahead and order since we're on a tight schedule," I said as I gave my tablemate the side-eye for being so time crazy.

"OK. What will it be?"

"Let me have the CP3 pancake platter with scrambled eggs - add cheese - and a side of Bowman Gray grits. And, let me also get two links of turkey Salem sausage."

"And what will be your culinary pleasure this afternoon?" Jermaine looked at Dayna like he was thinking about how pleasurable she would be.

"What did you say your name was again?"

"Jermaine, ma'am."

"Don't ma'am me. I ain't that old, young buck." Dayna flipped to page two of the menu and skimmed the bottom half with her middle finger.

"Yes, ma'am." Realizing his mistake, Jermaine shared a kind smile and waited patiently for her order.

"OK. Let me get the I-40 Showdown with some cheese eggs and some Bolton bacon."

"And to drink?"

"Two orange juices, please." Dayna answered then she picked up her phone to check for any missed emails.

"Sure thing. Coming right up. Please make yourselves at home and if you need anything, and I do mean anything, please do not hesitate to let me know." He gave Dayna a stare that told her that he could be her anything. For a youngin' he sure had guts. We laughed about it after he left to place our orders.

I didn't waste any time finding out what all the hush-hush was about. My curiosities were getting the best of me.

"So, girl, tell me what this is all about?"

"You just can't wait, huh?" Dayna nudged me playfully.

"No. Now, come on. Tell me." I stretched my eyes so wide I looked like a contestant on the Price Is Right waiting for the curtain to open.

"OK. First, let me say this. I want to let you know how proud I am of you for the success of your business. You are one of the hardest working women I know, aside from me and Synatra, and I just want to say that I love you and I admire you for all that you do. You are always so busy taking care of everyone that you never take time for yourself."

I listened with heartfelt ears as Dayna continued, but couldn't help myself to respond. "Yes, I do."

"No, Vay, you don't. You do so much for everybody else that you often neglect your own happiness. You've committed your life to looking after me and Syn and I don't think we've ever really took the time to say 'thank you'. You mean the world to us", she continued, as she reached for a tissue in her purse, "and I just want to say 'thank you, Vay'. I love you."

She reached into her jumbo-sized Michael Kors handbag and retrieved an ivory-colored envelope and slid it across the table.

"What's this, Dee?" I questioned as I cautiously reached for the envelope.

"Open it, silly."

I tore into the envelope and gasped a breath of excitement. "No, you didn't, Dee. No, you didn't!" I exclaimed as I held my heart with my hand. In sheer surprise and excitement at the contents of the envelope, I shook my head in disbelief.

In my hand was a travel itinerary from the Dream Away Travel Agency detailing a five-day, four-night all-expense paid, all-inclusive Caribbean excursion to Aruba. Having never been out of the country before, I couldn't wait to explore this foreign opportunity. The enclosed brochure highlighted a two-bedroom deluxe suite at The Westin Aruba Resort. Also included was a gift card for up to 12 hours of luxurious spa services.

Thoughts of turquoise gleaming waters that waved under the Caribbean sun gave me pause as I closed my eyes, took a deep breath and pretended to breathe in the island air.

I noticed on the airline ticket that the flight was scheduled to depart at 11:00 am one week from today and that escalated my excitement even more. It was true and I had to admit to myself that I had given much to my family, especially my sisters, although I would never admit this to them. But, I did so because it was the right thing to do. Being the middle sibling I somehow had become the caregiver, nurturer and leader. Family was family and no matter what they always came first. Besides, they would do the same for me if the shoe was on the other foot, right? Not wanting to be the one to seek validation or a medal for my many years of sacrifice, I kept that admission to myself.

All kinds of thoughts were running through my head. What to wear, what to pack. I even wondered if I was within the timeframe so I could submit a 'mail hold' with the post office. The office would have to be appropriately scheduled since I was planning to be gone for an entire week.

"You're right, I didn't. We did!" At that moment, Synatra had joined us at the table.

I could hardly contain myself as I slid from the booth and stood to hug my baby sister.

"Hey, baby girl! What are you doing here?"

"Surprising you, girl. What you think?" Synatra slid into the booth next to Dayna and hugged her in the process.

"Y'all what is all of this?" I asked looking between both siblings. Synatra was the first to speak up as usual.

"What it look like? We sendin' you on a vacay, and a real one at that. You need to let your hair down or take it off and sit it beside you or something." I leaned over laughing while Dayna just shook her head at the ratchedness that always seemed to find its way out of our sister's mouth. "You becoming too much of a lame-o, girl. Loosen up!" We all laughed because her statement had a hint of truth to it and we all knew it. "Besides, I know Dee did her whole marketing pitch as usual, so I'm just gonna say what I gotta say. We love you, Vay, and we want you to get away and have some fun." Synatra flailed her hands in the air as if she was stirring up some commotion. "And, it wouldn't hurt if you and Stella over here went and did y'all thing on the island. Well, maybe not you, Stella since you got the band on the hand and thangs," she said referring to Dayna's marital status.

Confusion settled on my face. "What do you mean, me and Stella?"

"'Cause I'm going with you!" Dayna whipped out a second envelope that contained the same travel information as me. A simultaneous screech was shared between us that directed all eyes on us.

"Wait. What about you baby sis?" I took notice that she didn't reach for anything. Instead, she just leaned on her hand and rested her elbow on the table.

"Girl, I can't leave the empire right now. These fools ain't no-where-near trustworthy for me to leave them for a whole week. If I go wit' y'all I'm liable to come back to total chaos and you know that's not how I gets down when it comes to the business." Dayna nodded in agreement, understanding Synatra's hesitation. But, I pushed the envelope a bit further.

"Things look like they are running OK to me."

"That's because I'm here. Taryn has only been here a few weeks and Jermaine wants to sop up every woman he sees with a biscuit – a biscuit he probably ain't paid for might I add – and he is just not focused enough for me. Rosalyn has her head too deep in the numbers to come up for air. Adrian hasn't learned all there is to know, but he's getting there."

Jermaine was a junior at Johnson C. Smith University, the city's only HBCU. The only reason he worked was so he could earn a little paycheck to try to impress every woman he saw. To him, having a job and going to school qualified him as qualified. If only he knew.

Adrian was hired three years ago as a dishwasher and currently works as one of the shift managers at night. Synatra was always impressed with his ability to delegate and execute so it didn't take her long to realize that he had a few hidden talents. She also learned that he was skilled in the kitchen. She simply didn't want to place him in a position of temptation. He had a little more to prove to her.

Hell, they all did. He was definitely on his way to becoming partner material, but he wasn't there yet.

Seeing this, she pitched the idea of him certifying his abilities with a degree. She would write off the tuition cost as an educational expense. At his acceptance, she made arrangements for him to attend Johnson & Wales Culinary University. With all of his gifts, the one thing that stood in her way of leaving Adrian to operate solo was the fact that he was a convicted felon. Any other convicted felon wouldn't have been allowed to set foot on the doorstep, but this was her spot and she could run it the way she wanted to and with whom she wanted to run it.

She knew a lot of people, but she also knew a lot of people who could get stuff done. Like the Dean of Enrollment Management.

Dr. Janine Brady, was her former cosmetology instructor from the community college. They had kept in touch over the years and had become the best of friends. Besides, J&W had a reputation of churning out the best and only the best. They had a two-year waiting list at the time he applied, but he definitely didn't have to wait that long.

"Besides him, no one else in here can go at this with the same amount of love and passion that I bring, ya dig? Everybody else is just in it for the paycheck, but that's all gonna change once I work on this restructuring plan. I might need your help, sis." She looked towards me and dipped her head. "Until I can get them up to speed and without having to quarterback this thing, I gotta stick around, shawty."

Just then, Jermaine returned to our table and carefully placed our food before us, positioning our food so that the main course was closest to the edge of the table just as he was taught while taking his etiquette education certification. One would have thought he was putting on for us because Synatra was sitting at the table. We didn't mind, but Synatra was definitely checking out his service technique. She was checking to make sure he went by the book as was instructed during employee training and orientation.

Rising to leave, Synatra said, "Well, I'ma leave y'all to these scrumptiously tasty and delicious dishes y'all just chose." Then she asked, "What y'all doing when y'all leave here?"

"She hasn't told me yet," I shared, pointing my fork in Dayna's direction.

"She'll be alright" was all Dayna could say. Synatra gave each of us a departing hug and retreated to the back of the restaurant.

We finished our meals as much as we could. As usual, Dayna needed a to-go container so she summoned for Jermaine to come back to the table. Just as he was delivering the crate, Dayna's phone began to ring. While she answered her call, I dug out my compact and double-checked the status of my face. Seeing no crumbs, I reapplied my MAC Juices and Berries lip gloss, breaking a cardinal dining etiquette rule, and sat back to let my food settle a bit.

"OK. Sounds good. Thanks for calling." Dayna ended her call and emptied the remaining contents of her plate into the box.

"Who was that?"

"Don't worry about it. Come on before we're late." Dayna grabbed her purse, dropped a fifty on the table and eased out of the booth.

The closer we got to the car, the more intense my need to question her again became. So, I asked her again. "OK, chick. Where are you taking me? If you won't tell me the truth, the whole truth and nothing but the truth, at least give me a hint." I playfully threw a childlike temper tantrum.

"Let's put it this way. I'm taking you somewhere special to get you a special treat and when we leave you will come out feeling like a special new woman." Dayna pressed the unlock button on her key fob and we both got in.

"Well, I guess we're going shopping then. I'm glad I wore some comfortable clothes and shoes then."

"Shopping? Well, you can say that." And with that, Dayna popped her gear in drive and sped away from the curb.

Chapter 2 - Dayna

A smile crept on my face as I thought about the surprise I had waiting for Vay. I loved my sisters dearly and there were no limits to the things I would do for them. Well, maybe except kill someone, but the only exception to that rule was if it was a no-good boyfriend of one of theirs who had done my sister wrong.

"What are we doing here, Dee?"

Nevaeh just had to know everything. Here I was trying to surprise her with a little R & R and all she kept doing was asking a million and three questions. But, that was my sister though and I wouldn't have it any other way.

I found a park just in front of the salon, so I claimed that space as my own and killed the ignition.

"Vay, let me do something special for you, OK? I want this trip to be one of the best trips ever. You deserve it. Just know that you're in good hands."

"See, now you're starting to sound like that fine Dennis Haysbert on those Allstate commercials." Nevaeh laughed. "OK. Let's do this."

***

Several hours later we were both sitting under the ultraviolet dryers waiting for our gel manicures and pedicures to set. I chose a neon rose pink and Vay selected a galactic turquoise with a funky striping design on her ring fingers and big toes. This was much spunkier than her usual professional looking white French tips. We both looked brighter in the face thanks to a lovely facial and hot eyebrow wax. Sometimes I thought Leisa applied the wax when it was too hot, but I guess the hotter the wax the stronger the bond.

I gave my digits one last look over and stood to stretch when Leisa reappeared from the back of the salon.

"OK, ladies. I am ready for you now." She turned to walk back down the hall way and entered the third room on the right.

"What's next? What is she ready for?" Nevaeh blew on her fingers and carefully eased her feet from under the light.

"Something special." I hugged her with the wet-nail approach. "And, it's about to change your life. Come on."

We made our way to the room to find Leisa sitting on her stool at a much larger station. In front of her was a masseuse table, covered in crisp white linen. The room was much dimmer than the front of the salon and the music was much more easygoing. The lilac aroma adjusted my mood to prepare me for my next service.

"Here, ladies. Let me take your purse and make you more comfy, O-kaaay." Leisa smiled as she spoke in her native mandarin accent. I did one last wipe over my nails to ensure they were completely dry and took off my sandals. I lifted my maxi dress long enough to remove my underwear and placed them in the bag I had in my purse.

"Would you like a glass of wine? It's complimentary." Leisa gave a Vanna White wave to her left and waited for the order. Still smiling and nodding she said, "I have some warm towels over here for you if you like, too."

One look at Nevaeh and the expression of 'oh hell no' was written all over her face.

"I know we're not getting ready to do what I think we're getting ready to do?"

"Do you remember when you told me to keep my panties on when we left this morning?"

"Yep."

"Well, get ready to take *your* panties off and hop up on the table."

"I will not. Girl, what is wrong with you? You are one sick – and freaky – chick!" We fell into each other laughing.

"I know, girl. It'll be fun. Besides, my baby loves it!" It was true. Braylon loved when I got a fresh Brazilian bikini wax. And, I would go all out, too. From the rooter to the tooter. It felt great and it looked great…after the swelling goes down. Every woman should experience it once in their lifetime.

"You know what. I'll do it. You said loosen up, right. So, let's get loose." I was shocked and pleased at the same time. She was really beginning to understand that it was time to let loose and have fun for a change. In the blink of an eye, she had kicked off her disposable flip flops and removed her capris and thong at the same time. We were both standing there semi-naked.

I hopped up on the table first. Nevaeh looked on as Leisa slid on a fresh pair of latex gloves and prepped my cubby area. Her mouth was wide open. She looked on in disbelief and I could tell that she was indeed having second thoughts about her decision to go through with it.

"I can't believe you feel comfortable enough to lay there spread eagle with this woman about to snatch out every hair follicle you've ever grown down there." Leisa continued applying hot wax in large strips all over the left side of my lady lump.

Once the strip of linen fabric was applied and smoothed over, she quickly ripped it in the opposite direction. I screamed slightly as I have every other time I've had this service done. Even though it only took a split second, it hurt like hell. It was a pain that I don't think anyone could ever get used to. Especially not in that area.

Leisa finished the left side and proceeded to the right. And then to the landing strip. I had to ask Vay to turn around while she cleaned up my Hershey highway. I didn't want her to know me like that so I spared her emotions.

Once I was finished, I waited for the cooling gel and the skin moisturizer to be applied so that I wouldn't experience any skin irritations. I waited a moment longer before I sat up.

I always wore a dress because I didn't like the way the disposable undies felt after this kind of service. The dress allowed me to go commando for a little while at least until the pain subsided.

I stepped inside one of the private rooms where the walls were surrounded with mirrored views to make sure that everything that I didn't want there wasn't there. Seeing that I was as clean as the day I was born, I slid the curtain back and walked out.

"I can't believe I'm doing this." Vay was leaning against the wall shaking her head in total disbelief.

"You can do it, Vay!" I began to chant her name. *Vay, Vay, Vay!*

She didn't chicken out on me as I thought she would. She waited for Leisa to change her gloves and the linen paper on the table and hopped up on the table. She looked up and found that spot on the ceiling and stared intensely.

"This your first time, I see." Leisa was faced with a bush so thick she had to plant clips along the sides of her road to find her way to the palace. Knowing Vay, there was no need to clean up the palace that often since she didn't usually invite company over.

"Uh, when was the last time you at least shaved girl, dang?" I asked looking over at the forest she called a cha-cha.

"Don't judge me. Mind your business!"

"I never knew there really was such a thing as coochie cobwebs until now!" I laughed and she stuck her tongue out at me.

In an effort to reassure her that everything would be OK, Leisa grabbed a fresh packet of shears and ripped open the sanitary casing. She needed to trim down the area first before she could even begin. Poor Vay. She looked so embarrassed. I was embarrassed for her and I let her know it, too.

"You know, you really should do this more often. I mean, how do you ever expect a man to come see you if he can't find where you live?" This inquiry and reference to the almighty va-jay-jay eeked a slight laughter out of her. For the most part, she was concentrating and getting mentally prepared for what was about to happen.

Thirty minutes and two duck walks later, we were finally leaving the salon. Both of us were walking like we had a large fitness ball between our thighs. I could tell from the look on Vay's face that she felt some type of way about this particular first in her life. I waited a few minutes before we pulled off. For one thing, I had to get out one last laugh as I watched her climb into my truck.

While she was getting her treatment, I pulled out my cell phone and took all kinds of pictures of the funny faces she made after the first rip. She looked traumatized. I laughed so hard until I cried. I continued to scroll through the pictures flashing her the images that were taken.

"Dayna. I just thought about something. I'm not gonna be able to go - especially not for an entire week. I have a business to run and so do you."

"No worries. I have already made arrangements. Jessica is gonna hold me down and I've already talked to Syd about it. So, we're good." Sydney was Vay's partner in crime when it came to business. The two of them were like a double dose of Superwoman and Shera. They were definitely prosperous in their consulting profession.

The two of them had the market cornered. They received numerous awards and accolades and impressive recommendations from one business entity to the next. The City of Charlotte voted The Jones Group, Inc. as the number one ranked small business in Mecklenburg County for five consecutive years.

She didn't say anything after that. I could tell that she was very grateful and excited about the opportunity to not have to worry about anything. Seeing the calm on her face, I grabbed her hand, squeezed it and headed towards the north side to take her back home.

I pulled into the driveway and waited for Vay to gather her things.

"Alright, girly. You have exactly one week to get your affairs in order. After that, we will forget everything business and orderly. From the moment we leave for the airport, we are not considered business women. We are considered footloose and fancy free. "Woo…I can't wait!" I think I was more excited than she was at that time.

"You got that right 'cause Lord knows I need this break." With the last bag in her hand she exited the jeep and made her way to the garage door. She waived once she was in the house and I tooted the horn to signal my acknowledgement. I changed my mp3 track to some old school Mary J. Blige and nodded my head to *My Life* all the way home.

Braylon had beaten me home as I noticed the front door partially cracked when I pulled into the driveway. That wasn't like him to leave the door open. Just then, he was making his way down the steps and back to his car. He pressed the trunk release button on his key and removed several bags from the trunk. He looked like he didn't want me to see what they were so I played along and allowed him to make a dash for it back to the front porch. From what little bit I saw, it definitely looked like he a bag from The Pleasure Palace. It seemed to me like he was preparing to send me off with a bang – literally. I was in for a long week.

Chapter 3 - Synatra

The one thing I loved to do that not too many people knew about was run. I had joined the running organization specifically for black women more than four months ago. Rosalyn Bennett, my newly hired accountant, had invited me to attend one of the meet-ups with her one Thursday. She said she got into it because somebody invited her and so on and so on. At first I thought running was strictly for weirdos and white people, but what I have found is that running helps me to clear my head and come up with new ideas for the restaurant. I felt better, I breathed better, and I damn sure looked better. The ass I had built was nothing short of a miracle. I had 'back' before, but now I have one of those asses that make a stripper say 'damnnnn' like Smokey and Craig on *Friday*. Five miles in, I turned around at my usual spot and headed back towards the house.

When I got back, I ran upstairs to prepare for my shower. I was scheduled to be at the restaurant in two hours so I had to move fast. Rosalyn was preparing to brief me on our financial situation for our quarterly meeting and I needed to be prepared for any and all information.

My plans were to go and discuss the report and then engage in a little retail therapy. Anytime I talked about money made me want to spend a little money to relieve some of the stress.

I slipped on a pair of Seven jeans and hooked it up with an emerald green cashmere cardigan. I paired my look with a matching scarf and a pair of five inch chocolate brown leather Jimmy Choos boots. Each hair on my head was in the right place and my makeup was a mural of perfection. I grabbed my keys and my purse and headed for the garage.

It was time to take my new baby – a 2014 Jaguar XF – for a twirl. It was a nice little gift I bought for my twenty-fifth birthday. Who cares if I still had three more years to go?

I strolled past the Southpark Mall making my way to the highway. Having my business in uptown Charlotte was gravy, but traffic could be a bitch at times. As usual, I parked in my reserved parking space adjacent to the main office of the EpiCentre. Before things got to be too hectic, I checked my Facebook wall one last time to make sure I hadn't missed anything. Sometimes a little ratchet entertainment was all I needed to give my day a boost.

There weren't enough compartments in the world that would be too much for a woman's handbag. My keys always seemed to get lost yet I would find them in the same place every time, but luckily the door was already unlocked. My phone hadn't buzzed with an alarm alert, so I wondered who could have beaten me here. I thought maybe Rosalyn was in the back somewhere so I called her out. She didn't answer.

But, Adrian did.

Adrian had arrived at work earlier than usual. In fact, I mentally recalled his schedule and remembered that he wasn't supposed to be at work until six this evening. Here it was eight in the morning and he was working like we had a full house.

"What'chu doin' here, Adrian? Thought you wasn't coming in 'til six?" I placed my handbag on the barstool and tossed my keys inside. The smell of fresh coffee led me to the end of the bar.

"Good morning, Ms. Jones." He wiped his fingertips off on the little towel on his shoulder and reached for a mug. "I came in a little early for your meeting. Coffee?" he asked slowly pouring me a cup of brew.

"Nah. I'm good."

"Suit yourself." He added a bit of amaretto cream and sugar to the mug and drank the coffee himself.

"Roz here yet?"

"No, ma'am she's not."

"You got something in the oven back there?" I looked around him in the direction of the kitchen.

"Yes, I do."

The smell that had gotten my attention was a Bavarian cream French toast bake. On one of the dining room tables, laid two plates with vegetable frittatas adorned with a sprig of fresh parsley. The fruit bowl centerpiece played host to the carafe of freshly, squeezed grapefruit juice and other accompaniments for the spread.

"Wow. This is quite some breakfast feast you got here." I leaned closer to the platter and inhaled. "Smells good. And, I'm hungry, too!"

"You're very welcome, Ms. Jones."

"Look, look, look. We already talked about this Ms. Jones-thing, a'ight. You can call me Synatra. It's cool, ya know."

"Indeed, Ms. –" he quickly corrected himself, "Indeed, Synatra."

"That's more like it. Come sit down and chop it up with me for a little bit before Roz gets here." I patted the chair next to me and placed my napkin in my lap. Instead, he poured two glasses of juice and returned the carafe to the chilled platform on the table.

Before I could finish chewing the first forkful of food I offered, "Damn, this is good. I almost forgot how good of a cook you was."

"I'm glad you're enjoying it. I just thought I would prepare breakfast for the two of you before you began your meeting. I know how stressful it can be when it comes to the numbers."

No he didn't. It was one thing to cook for a sister; it was another thing to be in my mind and thinking just like me. The fact that he knew what we were up against turned me on. All the way on.

"Besides, I wanted to surprise you with this recipe I'd been trying out."

I hardly listened to him as he schooled me on his trials and errors for perfecting the dish before me. Every word he spoke seduced me into a daydream. Damn. I never noticed before but he was sexy for an ex-con, as if his social classification really mattered. He was what I called a 'professional thug'. You know the kind that could go from the board room to the basketball court, only on *his* court, his teammates had been murderers, rapists, and drug traffickers and not point guards, forwards and centers.

I literally tried to stare a hole into his shirt, carefully scanned him from top to bottom. His covered physique appeared to have all the right muscles in all the right places and I do mean 'all the right places'. I pictured him wearing a gray beater with a pair of crispy black, Levis jeans. Throw in a pair of fresh wheat colored Timbs and you got a rough neck. He was the kind of rough neck that I could imagine doing me in the morning, at night. Hell, he could just do me and I wouldn't have cared what time of the day it was.

"Ms. Jones. Ms. Jones." He placed his hand on top of mine to get my attention. What did he do that for? I instantly felt an unsaintly shiver in my spine and a likening pulse in other places, too.

"What?" I finally broke from my stupor and snatched my hand back. This was the first time I was focused on what he was saying since I sat down.

"Ms. Jones, I just wanted to make sure you were OK. I seemed to have lost you at some point during my conversation. I hope I wasn't boring you." *Not at all thickety-thump-thump.*

"Nah, you wasn't, but I can see that I am not going to win this Ms. Jones-battle with you so you go 'head and do yo' thang. I'm good wit' it." Just then Rosalyn walked in the door and locked it behind her.

"Hey, y'all. What's going on? Oh, something smells good in here!" She hung her coat in the closet next to the wait stand and joined us at the table.

"What's up Roz. My man Adrian here hooked us up for our meeting. Thank the man."

"Thanks, Adrian." She leaned over to get a whiff of the breakfast bake and sipped from her glass of juice in the process. "You really out did yourself."

"It's no problem." I'm going to finish setting the front end and reviewing the inventory while you lovely ladies take care of business. I'll be in here if you need me. Enjoy!" With that, he turned around and walked that smooth cat-daddy walk that I loved to enjoy.

Roz and I looked over the books and surprisingly we were in better shape than I thought. I was impressed by her talent for always looking for the white space in our operations. She had managed to find ways that saved us approximately seventy-five thousand dollars in untapped reserves. At her suggestion, we discussed using those funds to reach out to form a partnership with a few of the local non-profit organizations that managed people who were homeless as a part of our new social engagement marketing strategy. Basically, we would package any food we had left over at the end of business each day and donate it to the shelter for the displaced. Along with that, she proposed a plan to host "Soup or Bowl" Sundays where members of the community could either make soup bowls for us to donate to the shelter or provide financial support and enjoy free bowling for a spring fundraising outing. The plans she laid out were straight fab and I was loving it. If we kept this up, I could almost triple my volume of business in less time than I previously projected. Admittedly, that line of thinking was before bringing her onboard with my team.

But, that wasn't even the icing on the cake. She figured out a way that we would decrease our taxable income by building a stronger relationship with the State of North Carolina Department of Public Safety in a joint effort to reduce recidivism. It turns out that businesses that hired convicted felons that have re-entered society received some fat tax credits. The longer we could keep their asses out of trouble, the more credits we received. I was all for it. I could give back to the community by *trying* to make them successful, contributing members of society while putting some more cheddar in my pocket and back into my business. Maybe I would be able to hire a few more faces and give some significant holiday bonuses to my current staff. Who knew?

"Thanks, Roz. This is some real good work, ya dig."

"That's what you pay me for. I'm happy to be of service to you and your establishment and thank you for giving R&B Accounting Services a chance."

"Fa show. You did your thing and I'm pleased." Roz went to get her coat out of the closet. "So, you're off next week on your vacation, right?

"Yes, I am. It's my Grandmother's birthday. She'll be eighty-five. She is going to be so pleased to see all of us there" she said swinging her jacket around and put it on. "I can't wait to see her."

"No need to explain. So, I guess we won't see you until next Monday then, huh?"

"That's right, but remember, I'm only a phone call away if you need anything. And just so you will know, I have already set up the direct deposits for this pay period and prepped the files for the upcoming payroll."

"You ahead of the curve, lady." I gave her a hug and patted her back. "Don't worry about us here. You go and have a ball with your fam. Y'all party hard and, ay, do the stanky leg with your grandmother for me, will you?" I leaned and strutted my leg to my own rhythm. Roz laughed at my gesture.

We walked to the front of the house, laughing and finishing a few sister-girl thoughts.

After she left, I locked the door back and made my way to the inventory closet to find Adrian. He was focused on counting the items on the shelf and comparing his findings to the numbers he had on his clipboard. I stood there a split second to admire the view. "So, Adrian. Can I ask you something real?"

"Sure. Go ahead." He stopped reviewing the list and rested the clipboard into his gut.

"Why did you really come in early this morning?"

"Why do you ask?" *Answering a question with a question, huh?*

"Because if I were a betting woman, which I'm not, I would have bet that you came in early because you knew that I would as well." I paused and waited for some type of reaction. There wasn't one. "Not only that, I would have bet that you knew I would be here early and that you would have wanted me to. Does that sound about right?" I leaned against the door frame and propped my foot up behind me.

"Ms. Jones? Did I offend you by coming in early? Will my early arrival somehow mess up your books because I didn't clock in?"

"Nah. Nothin' like that. I was just wondering."

"As my supervisor, I feel that it is only right that I be honest with you. I came in today because, yes, I knew you would be here early and I knew that the two of you would have been here by yourselves. I didn't want that so I thought I should come in and be a gracious host to y'all since y'all have been nothing but like family to me."

"So, what about your –"

"There's one more thing and I hope this admission doesn't place me in a bad light with you. But, I woke up in the middle of the night and couldn't go back to sleep. Truthfully, I'm still adjusting to life on the outside so, after a while I just decided to come on in and get a head start on things."

"Is that right?" I questioned intently.

"Yes. I enjoy working here and I love what I do."

Hearing the truth – hopefully – had a way of settling you. I admired a man who was a man, and an honest man just did it for me.

"I see. So, if you don't mind me asking, you don't have anybody in your life that takes care of you?"

"In what way do you mean?"

"However you need to be taken care of." I asked with a hint of sensation in my voice hoping he would get the hint. I tried hard not to let my horniness show, but from the look on his face I could tell I was quickly losing that battle.

"If you're asking me do I have a significant other the answer would be 'no'. I can't see me bringing a woman to my place right now. That's no place for a queen to be. So, I am just working to better myself and to build a home so that when I do find the right woman – and I will find her – I can provide for her and protect her like a man is supposed to. The funny thing is, sometimes I feel like that woman and I have crossed paths before and I hadn't recognized her. But, I have to do my part to prepare a home for her or someone else will."

He looked at me with a knowing look. Hearing this made me wanna dig a little deeper. Not to be nosey – sort of – but to get to know more about him. I don't recall ever thinking of a co-worker, let alone a subordinate, in this way before. But he intrigued me. He had a sweet mystery about him that called out to me and I just had to answer it.

"What about family?" He looked at me then looked down at his clipboard as if I was asking too many questions. I suppose I was, but at that time I really didn't care.

"Ms. Jones, if it's alright with you, I'd like to go ahead and finish the inventory assessment so that I can order the things we need. You do remember that we have an engagement party of forty coming in on Friday night, right?"

"Yeah, sure. Wedding party of forty on Friday." With that, he returned to the storage room and continued his count.

Later that day, I went into the main office and shut the door. I swiped the unlock code on my S4 and noticed that I had a few missed calls and a few missed text messages so I checked them. One of the voicemails was from Dayna. She called to tell me that she and Vay were on their way to the airport. There was another one from Vay saying that they had made it to Aruba and joked about me not calling them while they were away. I laughed and continued to check the rest of my messages. I saw nothing important, so I logged in to Facebook to check out my bookers to see what was going on with them.

Facebook had added a few new features that allowed you to see who had checked out your profile and how long they were on there. I liked it in a way and in other ways it was a bonafide stalker stopper. There was no telling how many people were just feening to click on an old friend or an ex's page to get the latest scoop. I had been guilty of it myself a time or two. It's not like I wanted either one of them back. I just wanted to know, to see if they had mentioned me. And, maybe a part of me wanted to know which tramp they might have been dealing with because I know none of them could compare to me.

The other hoes they were probably messing with ain't 'bout that life of a dime-piece like me. I keeps myself tight and them bum ass wanna be leftovers of lovers knew it. Some of them had been checking me out a little bit here and there, but none of them were worth the energy to block them. They could check all they wanted to. I'd been there done that. But one thing they couldn't do was say they saw me in their log because I figured out a way to block my information from ever showing up. A few key strokes here and there and my searches became invisible.

The list on the left-hand side listed several of my regular facers, but I didn't recognize the name or the profile of the last person that visited my page. I figured maybe, whoever she was, had the wrong person or thought she knew who I was or something. Somebody is always telling me that I look like somebody they know.

Since she was perceivably digging through my page I decided to return the favor and dig through hers. Anonymously, of course.

The intruders name was Season McCall. Pretty name, I thought, and from the looks of the pictures she had posted, she was a very beautiful woman as well. She looked like a model even. Her profile picture mirrored that of one of those celebrities that endorsed L'Oreal products. Her long, sun-bronzed color tresses wrapped around her shoulder and brushed the top of her haltered dress.

I scrolled through the remainder of her page to see what I could see, but there wasn't very much given she had all of her information set to private and you had to send her a friend request to see any of the details.

I clicked back to my wall and read a few status updates. I saw where my girl Queen had invited me to her invitation-only birthday bash in two weeks at one of the newest nightclubs uptown called Conversations. I hadn't been to it yet, but I heard that it was absolutely, positively and unequivocally for the grown folks crowd and that you would definitely leave there with something to talk about. I indicated my intent and logged off my account.

"Adrian?" No answer. I grabbed my keys and walked towards the front door and yelled, "Adrian?"

This time he heard me. "Yes?"

"I'll be right back. I gotta run to the store. You need anything?"

"No, I'm good. I'll stay here and wait for the deliveries that are scheduled to arrive today."

"OK. I'll be right back." I bounced out the door and walked back to my car in the parking garage.

I was in a good mood after having met with Roz this morning. To celebrate just how much of an impact she had made, I turned my iPod dial to my girl and sang along, wishing I could have this moment for life.

Chapter 4 - Braylon

Dayna had come home a little earlier than I had expected. I had hardly gotten in the door good before she pulled up in the driveway. I tried to get all the bags out of the car before she got home. I hope she didn't see anything.

Unbeknownst to her, I had begun preparing dinner by fixing her favorite meal: prime rib with a homemade lemon-garlic whipped butter glaće, twice-baked potatoes, honey-glazed carrots and some fresh, steamed broccoli. I prepared a few lobster tails to add a little surf in the mix. A bottle of Liberty School red wine donned the center of the table next to a set of crystal goblets I had purchased when we were in Paris. I had gotten them for her as a gift along with a bottle of 1969 Sauvignon Blanc. The Blanc was to be opened for our 20th wedding anniversary and not a moment sooner.

The smoothness of Kem filled the air with the sweet sounds of love and lust as she approached the door. I moved quickly to help her with her bags and placed the sweetest kiss on her cheek.

"Baby. What's with all of this?" She walked further into the kitchen and gasped when she entered the dining room.

"Hand me your purse and the rest of your things." I placed them on the sofa and moved to shut the door all the way. "Come here, love. Tonight is going to be a special night."

"For what? It's not my birthday or our anniversary or anything?"

"No. It's neither. But, there is such a special occasion called 'just because I love my wife.'"

She blushed and dropped her head. I knew the tears would soon be falling, so I reached for her and held her close to me. We hugged and began to sway to the melodic sounds of 'can you feel it'.

"Come with me, love. Sit here," I said motioning for her to take her place at the table. I helped her with her chair as she carefully rested on the plushness of her personal seat cushion.

"You're too good to me," she said.

I smiled at her and grabbed her hand and replied, "No. You are good for me and woman, I love you with everything I am. I want you to know that I appreciate you, I honor you, I respect you and I love you so much." I wiped a small tear from her face and kissed her on the cheek again. Then, I kissed her softly on her full lips.

We ate dinner and talked about her upcoming trip. I saw how happy it made her. I wanted to make sure she knew that I supported her efforts to take her sister on a tropical getaway because she had talked about doing this for quite some time. I loved my sister-in-law just the same as she, and if Dayna was happy, I was happy.

After dinner, I laid another surprise on her. I left the room for a brief moment to run her a nice hot bath. I made sure her favorite candles were lit. I placed her bath pillow next to the reading ledge and prepared her bath towel, cloth and robe. While she bathed, I stacked the dishes in the dishwasher and set the cleaning cycle. Seeing that we still had about half a bottle of wine remaining, I grabbed our glasses and the bottle and made my way back to the bedroom.

She was already undressed by the time I got there. I must have startled her because when I opened the door she quickly spun around. Her nudity excited me.

I followed her in the bathroom and helped her into the tub. I lathered her loofah with her favorite coconut and shea butter shower cream so that I could bathe every inch of her body. I almost succeeded in completing my task, but the intensity between us got the best of me.

I stood before her and did what she had been doing visually since the moment she came home.

I removed my dress shirt, pants, socks and threw them in the corner. Seeing her mouth separate told me she was ready for dessert. I dropped my boxer briefs and stepped into the Jacuzzi sized tub with her. I reached for her and she obliged.

Cupping her melons, I began to tease each nipple with my forefingers and thumbs. Her body responded immediately as she slowly straddled my body one leg at a time. This allowed me to deepen our intimate exchange.

In a whisper, I expressed, "I am so glad you are my wife. I love you and I always will."

"I love you, too, daddy." We collaborated in a slow, wet tongue exchange. I showered her with a few more kisses on her neck as she reached for my growing spear. When I responded positively to her touch, she removed herself from her seated position, descended and slowly caressed my rod with a delicate tongue wrestle. I moaned in pure delight as she demonstrated her wifely love and affection for me.

I stood and attempted to pull her up with me. But, she had other plans. She forced me to sit on the side bench of the tub and aggressively finished what she started. I moaned, she groaned. She inhaled and I exhaled.

For the next hour or so, we ravished in each other's love like we were teenagers. By the time we had reached the end of our shift, we were pruned, the bubbles were long gone and the water was cool to the touch.

Chapter 5 - Dayna

The seven o'clock alarm went off and I was sure it would wake Braylon. But, he was still asleep. I guess so after the work we put in last night.

I retreated to the kitchen to fix a pot of coffee and to get breakfast started. I turned the TV on as I began to prepare a starving man's breakfast of pancakes, eggs, turkey bacon, beef hash, and some of my famous cream cheese grits. I removed a few pieces of fresh fruit from the fridge and began to prepare a small platter.

After I set the table, I made a shallow pan of dishwater to wipe my cooking area as I prepared our meal. As I began to wipe down the counters and dining room table, I thought about how lucky I was being married to Braylon. Last night had brought back memories of when we first met.

I had just come from my doctor's office after a four-hour long visit. It was on that day that I was diagnosed with being a type II diabetic. He had given me a lot of reading materials and other information that would offer support to my condition. I was devastated.

I remembered getting in my car and traveling to the local Wal-Mart to pick up the prescription that my doctor's nurse had called in. After I received my medication, I asked the pharmacist a few questions and made my way back to the car. I must have placed my purse on top of the car as I went to remove my car keys from my pocket, but I didn't even remember. I sat inside the car and cried like a baby. Sure, I wasn't the only one in the world to have type II diabetes, but that wasn't the hardest part for my acceptance of my condition. The hardest part was learning about how long I had been in this condition and the reason behind it. My past had caught up with me.

Dr. LeGare shared with me that I most likely developed this condition when I suffered with gestational diabetes when I was pregnant. No one had known I was pregnant, except for my doctor, me and Chris, my boyfriend from college. I hadn't even told my sisters although I was sure Nevaeh had expected something was wrong with me on several occasions.

For three days I lay unresponsive in a diabetic coma. From what I was told, I was found in the middle of the highway. Somehow, I managed to ease my foot off the gas pedal and the car slowed to a rolling stop. By His grace, I didn't hit anybody and no one ran into me. Cars just continued to honk and shout expletives because they thought I was some crazy old lady that may have mistaken the mile marker signs for the speed limit signs by decreasing my speed as I traveled in a 65 mph zone.

Because my oxygen levels had dropped dangerously low, I had to have an emergency caesarean section. I had given birth to a two-pound, ten-ounce baby girl, four months prematurely. Three hours after she was rushed to the NICU, the nurse informed me that she had succumbed peacefully in the middle of the night. I never even got a chance to see her.

Apparently, as Dr. LeGare had explained, I was suffering from a rare condition that caused me to retain my gestational status even though it developed while I was pregnant more than twenty years ago. He stated that there were only about five percent of black women that had ever gone through this condition. How lucky for the remaining ninety-five of the world's population of black women.

As I sat crying uncontrollably, there was a soft tap on my window. I gathered myself long enough to turn to see the most beautiful man I had ever seen in all my life.

He was very well dressed, tall and statuesque. Not too many men could wear a lavender skip-button, French-cuffed shirt and get away with it. But he was. I leaned away from the window and turned the ignition to on just enough for me to partially lower the window.

"Miss, are you OK?"

"No. No, I am not OK?" I continued to sniffle and sob.

"I see. May I ask you something?"

"Sure."

"I know you don't know me, but may I please ask you to step out of the car?"

"Are you the police or something? What? Is it against the law to cry in your own vehicle in a Wal-Mart parking lot?"

"No, no, no. It's nothing like that. But, I do want to hand you your purse that you left sitting on top." He tapped the roof of the car. "Again, may I ask you to step out of the car, please?"

"Why?"

"Please?"

"Sir, let me tell you something. I don't know you from a can of paint, but there is something about you that lets me want to honor your request. But, please know that I might not know karate, but I definitely know c-ra-zy. So, don't try anything."

He gave a humble grin.

I unlocked the door and he stepped aside to hold it open for me as I exited. Once I moved away, he looked at me and I looked at him. I didn't care that he saw my makeup running and my eyes bloodshot red. The next thing I knew, he took a step closer to me and I took a step back. With his arms invitingly opened, he took another step towards me and I accepted. He embraced me like he was exerting all of my cares away, and just when he did that, I began to cry again. I cried on his shoulder for what felt like an eternity. And all he did was let me.

I stepped back, realizing that I had ruined his shirt. "Oh, my gosh. I've made a mess of myself and ruined your shirt in the process. Please send me your dry cleaning bill and I'll take care of it." I took a deep breath.

"That's OK. Don't worry about it. I wanted to make sure you were OK. You didn't look like you were in any position to drive." He handed me a monogrammed linen handkerchief. Coincidentally, the initials embroidered on it were 'BMW'.

"Thank you, Mr. –"

"My name is Braylon Walters. Please, call me Braylon," he interrupted. "With whom do I have the pleasure of being in her presence?"

The material felt good against my skin. I lightly dabbed at the corners of my eyes and around my nose. I had no intention of sending the man off with a mucous filled piece of cloth, but I was so taken aback by my condition that I simply couldn't help the response that I just gave. "My name is Dayna."

"Evening, Dayna." He looked deeper into my eyes. "Dayna? Do you have a last name?"

"Jones."

"Well, it's very nice to meet you, Dayna Jones." He extended his hand waiting for a handshake.

"I can't shake your hand right now, not with all of this going on." I waived my hand in a centering gesture over my face.

"That's OK. I don't mind at all." He grabbed my hand anyway and smiled at me. His teeth were a dentist's dream. I imagined he could have been a smile model for an orthodontist's marketing strategy. The contagion of his smile made me smile back.

"Ms. Jones, how are you feeling now? Are you able to safely drive to your next destination?"

"Yes, I am." I gave his hand a light bounce. "Thank you, Mr. Walters. I really appreciate you taking the time to stop and check on me."

"Indeed." He reached into his pocket. "Ms. Jones, I know this may be in poor taste to the average person. But, I can assure you that I am far from it and from the touch of your spirit you aren't anywhere near it." He placed his hand in his pockets and took a business man's stance. "I would like to know if I can leave you one of my cards. Would that be OK?" he said as he flipped a card in front of me.

I took it and looked back and forth from it to him. "You're an attorney?"

"I am. Does my occupation offend you?"

"It does if you are using my behavior to assume that I must need some legal representation or something!" He chuckled at my insult.

"Ms. Jones. I am not looking for clients to represent, believe me. I just couldn't stand the fact of seeing someone as beautiful as you in your condition. I hate to see a woman crying. Really, I do."

"Oh, I see. Well, Mr. Walters, thank you for your card."

"May I have one of yours?"

"Sure." I reached into my purse and handed him one of my cards. He glanced at it and looked back at me. He later told me that he was very impressed with me. He recognized the name of my business, Sweet TempCakeTions, and remembered the label from a previous engagement. It seems that my bakery had provided the cake for his sister's wedding a few years back.

"Ms. Jones, may I call you some time?"

"You may."

"Great. I'll do that, but now, I would like for you to please enjoy the rest of your evening and be safe."

"You, too." After shaking my hand one more time, he turned and walked towards the front entrance of the store.

For the next eight months, I had talked to Braylon almost every day and had seen him just as much. After dating for nearly two years, he proposed to me. And, I'm not talking about in just some old ordinary fashion either.

I remember it like it was yesterday.

One of the things he learned about me was that my favorite place to be - other than in the presence of the Lord - was at the beach. The night before my thirtieth birthday, he took me on an exotic vacation to the Dreams Punta Cana Resort in the Dominican Republic.

After registering our bags for delivery and receiving our complimentary welcome drink from the concierge, we took a nice, relaxing stroll on the beach. It seemed like we were walking into the perfect sunset. I felt like I was living in a dream.

When we got back to the hotel room, I gasped in amazement at the live jazz band playing a soft tune in the living room of the penthouse. I recognized the sound as being that of 'So What' from Miles Davis' *Kind of Blue*. My nose was assassinated by the aroma of fresh vegetables and other delectables coming from the kitchen. To my surprise, *the* Chef G. Garvin was putting the finishing touches on one of his culinary creations, including his famous lemon egg nog mousse.

After dinner, I retreated to the bathroom for a self-indulging milk and honey bath that one of the personal assistants had already drawn for me. Braylon had left the room to escort the band and Chef Garvin back to the lobby to thank them for their services and chop it up for a bit. He was gone for almost an hour so I figured the manversation must have been pretty darn good.

I slipped into the silk, eggplant purple nightgown he'd laid out for me, brushed my teeth and gave my hair a few strokes before doing a quick facial. Just as I was about to lie down, he returned to the room and joined me on the side of the bed.

He grabbed my hand and got lost in my eyes for a moment. He said, "May I ask you something?"

"Yeah, sure. What's on your mind?"

"Do you love me?"

"Yes, baby. You know I do!"

"Can I hear you say that?"

"Braylon Malik Walters, I love you."

With a schoolboy blush, he said "Thank you. I just wanted to hear you say that." He left me and went to the other side of the house to take a shower.

The night was quickly coming to a close but before it did, he helped me off of the bed as we got down on our knees to pray. He said a prayer for me and I said a prayer for him.

"Let's get some sleep, baby. Tomorrow is your birthday and I want you to be well rested as you receive the blessing of another year of life." He kissed me on my forehead and held me securely in his arms. And that was the night I knew that we grew closer in intimacy than anything I had ever experienced.

To date, we had yet to enjoy the intimate satisfaction of one another and I was perfectly fine with that. I didn't want to imagine how he was able to survive the past twenty-four months, but he told me a long time ago that he was remaining celibate until such time as the Lord blessed him with a virtuous woman that he could make his wife.

Early the next morning, the doorbell rang, waking me out of a sound sleep. I reached to my left only to find that side of the bed cool and smooth. I slowly sat up and looked around, first wanting to know where Braylon was, and second to know what time it was. I reached to grab my robe that was conveniently placed on the accent chair adjacent to the night stand and made my way towards the door.

Braylon had beaten me to it.

Room service had delivered a scrumptious breakfast spread complete with two carafes of orange juice and a fresh pot of coffee. After we said the blessing, Braylon provided his remixed rendition of 'Happy Birthday' complete with a Stevie Wonder swag.

"Happy Birthday, baby!"

"Thank you, sweetie."

"Maaaan, have I got a surprise for you today!" Braylon smiled as he stuffed his mouth with a fork full of his vegetable omelet followed immediately by two big bites of toast and a huge gulp of juice.

"Slow down, greedy. You're going to choke yourself!"

"That will be quite alright with me because I know I have the perfect technician here to give me mouth-to-mouth." He jolted his eyebrows towards the north a few times.

"You're so silly. So, tell me. What's the big surprise?"

"Now, babe…if I told you –"

"I know, it wouldn't be a surprise," I said finishing his sentence. "But, sweetie, whatever it is, isn't it a little too early to get it?" The clock on the over-the-range microwave read six-thirty in the morning.

"Well, I figure we may as well get up and get dressed and be out of here soon 'cause our day officially begins at eight o'clock sharp. And, just as the human itinerary instructed, we finished breakfast and got dressed.

It was eight o'clock on the dot when Braylon opened the door. In the hallway, stood a tall, white gentlemen dressed like the butler from that TV show with the goofy, black guy. He was holding a large, velvet covered box with a huge red bow.

"Good morning, sir. Madame."

"Good morning," we responded together.

"Braylon, what is all of this?" The ceilings in the hallway were flanked with white, sheer coverings accompanied by little, clear white lights than extended the length of the walkway.

"This is a part of my surprise." He grabbed my hand with one of his and supported my back with the other.

"This way, please." "Geoffrey" turned towards the remaining doors and removed the top. As he led the way down the hall, he slowly began to drop red and white rose petals with each step. We followed closely behind him. He stopped in front of the first door on the right.

Braylon turned my face to his and kissed me on the lips. "Dayna, I remember the first day we met. It was in the parking lot at the Wal-Mart off of I-85. From that day and not a moment removed, I have loved you with everything I was made of. You have walked with me, walked beside me, walked behind to support me in everything I do, and walked ahead of me to protect me as only your angelic presence can. And, for that I say, 'thank you.'" At that moment, "Geoffrey" removed a key card from his pocket and opened the door. Out walked my parents. I was so surprised. I began to speak to ask them what they were doing there, but Braylon quickly yet respectfully shut me down. I was told not to ask any questions and to just go with the flow.

Behind door number two were the best sisters a girl could dream of. Synatra and Nevaeh were smiling so hard. They both hugged me and waited for us to begin to move again before joining our parents and following us down the long corridor.

One room after another and as Braylon continued to shower me with his love and memories of special moments we'd had together, dates we had been on, disagreements we unfortunately had, "Geoffrey" opened the door. Behind each door were immediate members of my family and immediate members and closest friends of his family. My closest friends from Winston-Salem, Greensboro, Chicago and Philly were even there. Jayson and Brian, his partners and their wives from his law firm and my staff from the bakery were there as well. I was really blown away to see my stylist and nail tech, Kanada, and her husband Charles there.

As we continued down the long hallway, everyone else followed in tow. One of the next to the last rooms was occupied by my pastor, Dr. Marks, and right across the hall from him was his pastor, Dr. Mosely.

He rented out the entire penthouse floor and paid for everyone to join us, all with complements of his priceless love for me.

We entered a huge skyview banquet room that gave the most impressive views of the island one could imagine. In the distance, you could even see the cruise ships traveling the seas.

A room full of roses greeted me. There had to have been thirty dozen red roses in there. But, the one that stood out to me the most was a massive bunch of white roses with a single red rose in the middle. Everyone gathered around me as Braylon released my hand and walked over to the white arrangement. He slowly pulled the red rose from the center of the bouquet and handed it to me. "Geoffrey'" had made his way over to retrieve a silver platter and stood next to him. When he lifted the top, on it was placed a small red leather box. Braylon retrieved the tiny chest and guided me closer to him so that everyone could see. He handed me the red rose and said, "Happy birthday, love." Everyone around shouted 'happy birthday' and I turned to show them my lucky-me smile. When I turned around, in one swift move, Braylon dropped on one knee.

I gasped.

"Dayna, there aren't enough words in the English language to describe the joy you bring me each day we are together. I thank God daily for your presence. Being with you is like a present God gave me to open each day. I want you to know that I have prepared a permanent place in my heart for you and in that space lay our God, you and me. I left a little room in case we ever decided to start a family!" We heard slight chuckles in between sniffles. "I am glad that you have allowed me to love you. I am ecstatic that you have shared your life with me. Baby, I don't know what the future holds, but I know I don't have one without you. I refuse to live another minute without knowing that I will be privileged and honored to wake up to you and only you every day for the rest of our forever. I believe that you were made for me and in turn for my obedience to Him, He sent me to find you that day. Please know that I love you and that love will never cease. So, today and at this time I ask you, Dayna Yvonne Jones, will you marry me?"

There wasn't a dry eye in the room, including mine. I had cried so much that my eyes felt like they were on fire. As he remained in his king-like position, I could see a single tear break free from the corner of his eye.

He removed the treasure inside, revealing a platinum, five-carat, asscher-cut diamond surrounded by at least another five carats worth of baguette diamonds, and held it above my finger of eternal love and commitment. Through soft sobs and trying to catch my breath, I happily said 'yes'.

He had made provisions for our wedding to be conducted at seven o'clock that evening and all of it was planned right under my nose. Immediately following the engagement luncheon, I journeyed from one appointment to the next preparing for my big day. After manicures, pedicures, and getting our hair styled, Synatra and Nevaeh shared another round of tears with me before we went to our final appointment of the day to get our makeup taken care of. I simply could not believe that someone could love somebody like me the way he had. After today, I would no longer be a member of the forty-two percent club – indicating that forty-two percent of black females had never been married. And, I couldn't have been more happy.

I was happy that he found me and I knew that God had sent him to me that day. I know this because he hadn't separated us since.

After our nuptials along the shore and as the evening air draped across our shoulders, we snuck off from everyone and shared a private moment of love and kisses.

I later learned that while he was thanking the musicians and the chef, he had met with everyone to go over the final details one last time. I figured that must have been what took him so long to come back to the room that night.

I also learned that I was the one that planned my entire wedding – sort of. He reminded me of a previous conversation we had when we first met when he inquired about my thoughts on marriage and family. After he refreshed my memory, I remembered our discussion.

Mostly, I recalled telling him that as much as I wanted to have a fabulous wedding, I was more concerned with the marriage than anything. To me, the wedding day would come and go, but the love, honor, respect and commitment would live forever with the two of us and God completing our third strand of life. Besides, I only planned to get married one time, and I was glad that he was the one to choose me.

I have always known that I was blessed to have a man like Braylon Malik Walters in my life and after experiencing the love we just made I knew it to be true forever and always.

"Dayna!" I hadn't heard Braylon awaken or enter the kitchen. I hadn't paid much attention to the bacon that I was burning in the oven either. "I've been calling you over and over. You OK, babe?"

"Yes. I'm fine. Sorry for burning the bacon." I opened the backdoor that led to the patio and propped it open.

"Here. How about you relax and let me make breakfast this morning."

"Thanks, sweetie." I retreated to the living room and turned the TV on. A re-run of *Celebrity Crime Files* was on so I watched and learned more about the downfall of the former hip-hop mayor of Detroit, Kwame Kilpatrick, as my husband worked his way around the kitchen.

Chapter 6 - Chance

Traffic at the hospital had picked up significantly. After all, it was the beginning of the summer train as we liked to call it. The summer train was when we got an influx of summer traumas at a rapid pace. This was mainly due to the fact that school was out and the city was full of bored teenagers with nothing to do and the only thing left for them to do was to do something stupid that would land them in my patient log.

Being the chief trauma surgeon, I had the honor of seeing it all and enduring it all. From the kid who jumped into a shallow spring causing his tibia to split his shin into two pieces - thus creating a seven-inch gap in his leg - to the old freaky couple that decided to make love on the roof of their house in the rain. Needless to say, they both slipped and fell twelve feet into their rose garden. We actually had one patient come in after she received a splinter. There were no limits to what came through the emergency department doors.

I headed back to my office to put the finishing touches on a memo that was set to go out to the trauma team. Because of the revised healthcare plan that was due to take effect in less than eighteen months, we had devised a plan that would allow us to remain ahead the curve. I knew that the changes that were proposed to take place would more than double the normal traffic we had at the center and we needed to be better than prepared. The change in the healthcare law couldn't have come at a worse time; I was scheduled to be out of the country for the next week.

The bruhs were slated to invade the islands in an effort to promote a new organizational initiative: The Brother's Reinvention Program.

Morgan, my old college roommate and frat brother, was one of the principal investigators for the grant that we received to conduct the program. We had been some ride or die brothers since '96. We, along with my other line brothers, got matching tattoos to symbolize our brotherhood, but for us, our bond was beyond measure.

Both of us received full scholarships, including room and board, to attend Morehouse College. The night before graduation, we made a pledge to rise to successful levels in our careers and use every bit of energy and resources we had to be constructive leaders and give back to our followers in a major way. We were a few of the lucky ones in a sense because we grew up with our fathers, but we knew far too many young men in school that didn't. Some of them completed a few years after we did. Some of them never finished their first semester.

It was then that we understood the significant impact that growing up in a fatherless home could have on a young man - especially a young, black man.

After we finished graduate school, I continued my studies at Wake Forest University for medical school and he continued his studies in law at UNC-Chapel Hill. Neither of us held any animosity towards the other for my being a Demon Deacon and his being a Tarheel. As far as I was concerned, we were Carolina born and bred and that was all that mattered.

He and I had worked tirelessly on the curriculum and the development of the overall assessment and evaluation. The determining factor for receiving more than half a million dollars was the fact that our proposal was aimed to mentor and transform the lives of minority males to prepare them to become productive members of society. One of the catalysts for our program success was that each young man would be assigned to one of the bruhs beginning in elementary school and that relationship continues to develop into adulthood. We have a strong belief that you had to get to them early enough to sustain their potential for success. A few of the key career development initiatives included the help of elementary- and middle-school teachers and program coordinators for local non-profit groups. It was big time and I couldn't wait to get to our annual convention to formally present it to the rest of the bruhs.

Just when I stood to make my way to the conference room the phone rang and stopped immediately. I thought Nia, my receptionist, must have picked up my line for me.

"Nia. What's going on with you?" I reared back in my chair and crossed my legs at the ankle.

"Hey, Dr. Mathis! How are you?"

"I'm doing well. Thanks for asking. So, tell me something good."

"Sure thing." I grabbed a pen and prepared to take notes. "I wanted to update you on your travel plans. I've booked your flight, early morning and first class of course. I've also taken the liberty to schedule an in-flight conference call with Dr. Himes at 11:30 am at which time you should just be over the Bahamas." She completed the rundown of my itinerary and we discussed the schedule of the events for the convention.

"OK. That all sounds good, but please make sure you schedule the service to pick up my dry cleaning. Use my AmEx to take care of it."

"Do you need anything else as it relates to your trip?"

Three beeps interrupted my train of thought. "No, that should be everything." I reached over to check my cell phone to see who just sent me a text. It was Morgan. "Are you going to behave while I'm gone?"

"Don't I always? I'm always on good behavior, Dr. Mathis!"

"Yeah, right. OK, well let me get out of here and get to this meeting. We'll catch up before I leave, OK?"

"OK. Everyone is waiting for you in the main conference room, sir."

"Sounds good. Just send my information to me via email." I grabbed my portfolio and the two file folders I had on the lateral cabinet.

Everyone was there waiting for me to brief them on the upcoming events for the next few weeks. Dr. Jennis Himes was the supervising ER doctor and Dr. Chris Fisher served as his supporting ER surgeon. I had my hesitations about leaving these two in charge of the ER during my absence. There had been bitter blood between them ever since Dr. Himes won the vote for his current position, for which Dr. Fisher was denied. I, for one, didn't mind that the votes worked in Dr. Himes' favor.

It wasn't every day that a subordinate, by position number and salary grade only, was the ideal team player. Dr. Himes was the type of cat that was always on top of his game. He always arrived at work on time and was very professional. He has handled my schedule many a days when my workload or some other important engagement came up that wouldn't allow for me to be present. He never had a problem stepping in and serving where service was needed. I knew that I could always, and I do mean always, count on him.

Now, Dr. Fisher on the other hand – not so much. His image was oftentimes subpar. Either his scrubs were wrinkled, soiled with last week's spaghetti sauce or both. And, just like his appearance, his attitude was all over the place. The way he spoke about all the women he claimed to have had over the years, never calling them by their government name, told me that he had some serious trust issues. He was never on time for anything and as much as I had warned him and schooled him about the importance of being punctual and professional, he never abided by that rule or any of the others.

The only rules he lived by were his.

On the day of one of the most critical cases the center has ever faced, he arrived in surgery thirty minutes late. We were scheduled to perform an open-heart procedure on a six-year old boy.

We continuously monitor the young boy's stats as he showed signs of congestive heart failure and his condition continued to worsen. Hence, he was elevated to a level ten. His blood pressure fell rapidly and his body temperature began to decrease at a steady pace. I only had two hands to work with, but that young man needed another set to get his vitals and the bleeding under control.

No sooner had we located the drain in his left artery, Dr. Fisher entered the room. He walked in in a sanitized position holding both forearms in front of him and sought the assistance of the medical technician to complete his attire and went to work. Within a matter of minutes, he pinched the artery with a weaver clamp and sutured the opening with a simple, two-strand butterfly stitch. Everyone was impressed, including me.

As it turns out, he had been working on this discovery ever since he read about a patient dying from the same condition at a medical center in Philadelphia about a year ago. Using his engineering mind, he figured out a way to correct the problem in a manner that was less invasive and would yield the least time for recovery, yet offer the best results during the course of life.

This act of miraculous medical ingenuity was the only reason why he was still a member of this medical team, of this facility. We had received numerous awards on his behalf as it was the first procedure of its kind. The procedure later became known as the 'Fisher Stitch' and would be used by surgeons all over the world.

My directives were delivered to the team in less than fifteen minutes as I worked swiftly to bring the meeting to a close. I left Dr. Himes to finish the rest of the agenda, and by the look on his face, I could tell that made Dr. Fisher very uncomfortable.

For some reason, he always had this arrogance about him that signaled that he was always up to something. I couldn't quite put my finger on it but, I didn't have time to try to figure it out at the moment.

When I got back to the office, I noticed a brown envelope on my chair marked 'confidential'. The handwriting on the outside told me it was from Nia. I placed the packet in my leather messenger bag, grabbed my coat and dry cleaning from the back of the door and headed to my home away from home to be with my second family.

***

I made it to the airport just in time to go through the final screening before my plane departed. While I was glad to see that security had been beefed up post nine eleven, it was equally as annoying sometimes to have to deal with the rudeness and attitudes of the TSA. I swear they must have found the meanest of the mean and did just the opposite of Donald Trump and told them 'you're hired.' I don't know where they found some of those people.

Needless to say, I settled into the wide, comfortable leather seat and buckled the safety belt. A short while later, the flight attendants were going through their safety routine and as usual no one paid them any attention. I often wondered what would happen if one day they didn't go through the motions of flight attending and something major happened. But, I quickly dismissed that line of thinking because this was neither the time nor the place for such a thought.

After we reached our altitude and we leveled off, I checked my watch to keep track of the time. I had about fifteen minutes before I was scheduled to speak with Dr. Himes about some training and development we needed to implement for the staff. I was pleased for the most part with all that we accomplished as a team, but I began to wonder about the many pieces of the puzzle that made up the nightly-nine crew.

I retrieved my AmEx card and swiped the headrest machine to pay for my call. The operator instructed me to press a few buttons to acknowledge my understanding of the charges that would be associated with the call as I waited to be connected. Jennis picked up on the third ring.

"Doc. What's up with you, man?"

"I can't call it. How's the flight so far?"

"Good, man. Good. Well look, I'm not going to waste any time telling you about the number of peanuts that have been reduced in the onboard snack pack so let me get right to it." He chuckled a bit. "You know that last meeting we had with the board of directors got me to thinking about a few things. With the collapse of the economy and the reversion of six million dollars, I can't help but to wonder how the powers that be are planning to make up for this deficit." I could tell that his attention was undivided by his silence. "The problem as I see it is they are going to have to recoup those dollars somehow. With the way the economic climate has shifted, I think they are going to recover some of the losses by reducing our workforce. Now, don't worry, doc. In my book, you're safe with me, but there are some players on the team that I think may not be so lucky and it's out of my hands. I'll do everything I can to save their positions, but you know how it goes. So, let's be proactive about this thing."

"OK. I'm listening."

"I think we need to bring in a consultant to do an overall assessment on our departmental needs and what impact we would feel should we lose a few positions. I think we at least owe it to ourselves to forecast the inevitable. Let's be sure to capture how our operations align with the overall mission and the latest strategic plan. Have someone in human resources send you the complete personnel files for all of our staff. I don't want to be blindsided if there is something in anyone's file that somehow slipped our purview. We need to move swiftly and aggressively because I would rather be proactive than reactive to the situation. Wouldn't you agree?"

"Yes, Dr. Mathis. I think you're definitely on the right track. I will also be inclined to know what legal implication this may cause with a reduction in force."

"What do you mean?"

"Well, with a smaller staff and the way the patient volume is projected to increase, that would mean that we would work longer hours and have a larger caseload. There would be longer wait times for patients in the ER as well. This type of stress and strain on an already overworked brain may cause more harm than good. It leaves too much room for error which could ultimately result in an increased volume of malpractice lawsuits. That's just my opinion. What are your thoughts on that?"

"Nice. I like the way you think. We'll speak some more about this when I am back in the country. In the meantime, do some research and let's go ahead and bring in a consultant to see what our options are. I want us to be all over this one because I have a feeling, a strong feeling, that something is about to go down. I value the team I have and I want to be sure I have considered all options in the event I am asked to make some very tough, yet necessary decisions."

"You got it, Prez."

"Alright. I'll see you in about a week or so. Take care." I hung up and waited for the email confirmation that the receipt had been sent and turned the call feature off.

Tonight and tomorrow night would be the only official working days for me, so as I read today's Chronicle, I drifted in thought to the last minute details I needed to finalize for my presentation tonight. The rest of the time I could just relax or catch up with the bruhs.

It was almost one o'clock. Morgan's flight was scheduled to arrive an hour before mine so he should already be there by now. My flight was due to land in about another thirty minutes or so. I couldn't wait to see him and catch up.

My contemplations were interrupted by the attendant. "May I get you anything else, sir?

"No. I'm fine. Thank you." She acknowledged me with a playful smile and proceeded to check on the other passengers.

THE SIDE EFFECTS OF LOVE

I finished reading the paper and gathered my things. The pilot announced that we had already descended about ten thousand feet and to prepare for landing. I lifted my seat back up and waited for us to touch down before I thanked my Creator one more time.

After deplaning, I made my way to the baggage claim to collect the larger of my two bags. The car service Nia had ordered was waiting for me curbside.

"Hello, sir. I'm Dr. Mathis."

"Hello, Doctor. I hope er'y ting was irie, ya know?" The driver spoke with a heavy Caribbean accent that mirrored that of a Jamaican.

Understanding what I could, I responded, "Sure. Everything was great." He took my bags, placed them in the trunk and held the door open for me. Soon, we were off to the main island.

It wasn't long before we pulled up in front of the most artistically engaging lodging monument. The columns on each side of the motorized double-sliding doors that bore the image of a sculpted goddess reaching for the skies greeted me as I stood before the entrance. The lobby was carefully characterized with Italian pearl marbleized flooring with colors of the Arizona sands to match. The floor to ceiling windows stretched high into the foyer at least eighteen feet. I noticed the double staircase that hugged the lobby area with a welcoming curve on each side of the concierge desk. The business center was outfitted with a large conference room table and phone pod in the center. Computers and printers outlined the space.

The front desk attendant smiled brightly as I approached the station that guided each traveler to a single file line.

"How may I help you today, sir?" I approached.

"Chancellor Mathis checking in, please." She clicked a few keys for what seemed like a hundred words per minute.

"I'm sorry sir. I don't have a reservation for you."

"Please, check again. I am here with the Phi Alpha Phi Brothers Conference."

"OK, Sure. Let me check under that group name." She sped up her typing speed to do another search. "Here you are, Dr. Mathis! It looks like you have been added as our valued guest of the day which comes with a complimentary upgrade to one of our executive suites."

"Great! Thank you very much!"

"My pleasure. Also, you will receive a premier guest package which includes a bottle of our finest champagne, a fresh fruit display, two complimentary meals at our five-star signature restaurant, two complimentary spa service packages with a value up to three-hundred dollars, two of our one-hundred percent, twice-spun Egyptian cotton cloth bath robes, and last but not least, a gentlemen's choice luxury item."

"Wow! With all of that, what else could you all possibly provide me that you haven't already listed?"

"Well, that sir, depends on your pleasure. But, please choose carefully. The only thing I need to know from you now is what size condom would you prefer?"

"Excuse me?" I was completely caught off guard with this question. Not because I didn't know the answer, but because I didn't want her to try to find out."

"The size you select will determine your gentlemen's choice selection. We have regular-sized ribbed with a warming lubricant, the gold packs and for the elite gentlemen, we have the black packs. You do know what the black packs are, don't you?" I still looked at her trying to determine just how serious she was. "Here. Let me help you. Step back and drop your pants. I'm a pretty good judge of status in that area. One quick look and I'll have you sized up in no time. Either that or I will just have to grab it and find out for myself. It's really your choice, and I hope you choose the latter."

I stood momentarily speechless, as I looked around the lobby and waited for a video crew to come running out from behind the large window treatments or palm trees that were placed at each corner. "This has to be some kind of a joke, right?" Just then, I turned and saw Morgan coming from around the corner near the business center laughing hysterically.

"Morg?"

"What's up, bruh?" We laughed and hugged each other, finishing our greeting with our signature handshake. By now, the attendant was laughing, too. "Man, you should have seen your face!"

"You know what, you play too much man. You haven't changed since college!" We gave each other a shoulder bump and snapped it up.

"I know, I know - just having a little fun. I had to do something to lighten you up. I know how tense you can be sometimes. Hey, thanks for being such a great supporting actress." He walked towards the front desk and shook the lady's hand. He tipped her a twenty and stepped back to me.

"Dr. Mathis, thank you for being so understanding. I was starting to sweat from trying to pull this thing off." She held her hand against her chest and breathed a sigh of release. "Here are your room keys and the details of your package upgrade. May I get you anything else, Dr. Mathis?"

"No, thanks. You have definitely done enough." We squeezed in one last laugh about the situation before Morgan and I headed off to the elevator quad. He and I exchanged room numbers and agreed to meet each other in the lobby in a few hours. Not long after my ride to the top, I placed the key card in the electronic lock and entered my upgraded living quarters for what I would come to know as home for the next seven days.

The Caribbean chamber looked like it belonged to a sports celebrity. The panoramic views from the floor to ceiling windows welcomed me to the heaven that I had dreamed about.

I stepped into the sunken living room to marvel at the sixty-inch LED flat screen TV that was posted over a granite framed fireplace. Making my way to the oversized bedroom, I placed my luggage on the occasional table in the huge walk-in closet. I made sure my clothes were hung properly and according to my intended schedule. The California king-sized bed exuded a warm invitation to catch up on some sleep. I decided to use my little bit of down time to review my notes for tomorrow's presentation, but I was sure to take note of the recessed lighting that shone just above the head of the bed.

I grabbed the remote control to retract the curtains, exposing a large wrap around style patio that spanned the bedroom, living room and dining room areas. The small bistro-style table set made for a nice quaint little space to clear my head and enjoy the turquoise views.

My stomach boldly reminded me that I was due for some nourishment, so I made my way to the kitchen to check out the offerings. The refrigerator was bursting with an assortment of beverages, fresh fruits and accompaniments. Not one for cooking while on vacation, I decided it was best for me to order room service so I placed the order, and plopped down on the sofa to channel surf a bit. The channel guide revealed a throwback basketball game between the Chicago Bulls and the Detroit Pistons were scheduled to come in about fifteen minutes.

I read the schedule that was on the coffee table to see what amenities were being offered during my stay. There were a few interesting things that caught my attention. Time permitting, I would check out a few events, but for the most part I just wanted to relax and let the tides of the sea mist take my stressors away.

Just when I was attempting to relax my mind I remembered the envelope Nia had placed on my office chair. I decided I'd better call her one last time to remind her about that briefing I needed for her to complete.

"Thank you for calling The Mathis Office – this is Nia. How may I help you?"

"It's doc."

"Good morning, Dr. Mathis. Aren't you supposed to be on the islands by now?"

"Oh, I'm here. But, I wanted to update you on my conversation I had with Dr. Himes' this morning." I told her the details surrounding the conversation and welcomed any questions she may have had.

"Don't worry, Dr. Mathis. Dr. Himes has already briefed me. I kind of figured we might be heading in that direction, so I took the liberty to do a little research on my own. Didn't you get the envelope that I left for you?"

"Yes, I did, but I haven't had a chance to open it. Let me go and get it now?" As I walked towards the closet to retrieve it from my carry-on there was a knock at the door.

"Room service."

I liked this hotel already. Complimentary room upgrades, fast and efficient room service, comfortable living accommodations. I would have to be sure to add them to my top three vacation list.

"Hey. Let me get the door. We'll finish this conversation when I return, OK?"

"Sure thing."

"Oh, and Nia?"

"Yes?"

"Go ahead and take the rest of the day off. Tell doc before you leave though."

"Thanks, Dr. Mathis! Enjoy your conference."

"No problem." I grabbed my wallet and headed for the front door. After receiving my order, I handed the deliveryman a twenty and thanked him. He smiled as I closed the door.

The smell of the pineapple grilled chicken salad and cinnamon cheesecake hurried my pace to the dining room table. Ten minutes later I was releasing some pressured air from my chest. I laughed at the thought of what my uncle used to always tell my cousins and me when we were kids – excuse me, excuse me from the bottom of my heart, if it came out the other end it would have been a fart.

Memories.

It was almost three so I decided I'd better get changed for my meeting with Morgan. I looked forward to catching up with my buddy. I was sure he had new pictures of the family in his wallet that he just couldn't wait to brag about, but at the same time I couldn't wait to see them.

An hour later, I was dressed and heading out the door. Just before the door shut, I stepped back in to grab my cell phone from the charger on the kitchen counter and made my way to the lobby.

Chapter 7 - Nevaeh

There were exactly sixty-three minutes that stood between me and the moment I took off for paradise. I combed the house looking for any last minute items I would need. Remembering that the season finale of my favorite TV show, *Hour Conversations* was scheduled to come on next Tuesday, I set the DVR to record. I wheeled the larger of my bags to the front door and placed my traveling outfit across the bed next to my purse and carry-on bag.

After my shower, I got dressed and did my makeup. I had to re-do my eyes about four times because I was so anxious to leave I couldn't hold my eyeliner steady. This would be the first time I had been on vacation in about four years. That is entirely too long for a woman like me that puts in timeless hours for the progression of her business and as a result of my dedication, I had been become downright boring.

I gathered the rest of my things and placed them next to my suitcase at the front door. After canceling the alarm, I opened the door and checked the mailbox one last time. The only thing that was in there was the light bill and what looked to be an invitation to some event. That only meant someone, somewhere wanted something. The only thing I was willing to give was of myself when the sounds of the ocean took me away into an aquatic bliss. So whatever request was in that envelope would have to wait until my return, and that's if I ever came back.

At a quarter 'til ten on the dot my sister, with her punctual self, was turning into my driveway. All you could see was all thirty-two of her teeth and all you could hear were the sounds of Johnny Kemp talking about how he'd just gotten paid.

"Girl, turn that down! You gonna scare my neighbors!" I shouted at her as she clicked the trunk release button and helped me with my bags.

"A little bumping and thumping ain't never hurt nobody. It's probably what they need to hear to loosen up just like you." We laughed as she broke out into doing the butterfly dance. She looked more like a funky chicken trying to hail a New York taxi.

"Well, whatever. At least turn it down until we get out of the development."

"There you go. Stop worrying about folks. We are going to leave here and have a good time. Leave the worrying right here at the corner 'cause in the words of Sweet Brown, 'ain't nobody got time for that!'" We laughed something terrible as she sped out of the driveway and down the street heading for the airport. We called the 'rents and let Synatra know that we were on our way to Charlotte-Douglas International.

***

The flight from Charlotte to Aruba was priceless. Because Dayna was a frequent flier, racking up more than 300,000 miles with over 40,000 bonus miles, we were upgraded to first-class, compliments of the airline. Champagne and fresh fruit salads were offered as our in-flight snack. I was sure to get me a few packets of peanuts and dried fruit and Dayna got a few packages of mini muffins and some of those tasty biscotti cookies in anticipation of our nightly cravings.

As we descended before the runway, the flight attendant made an announcement that we should return to our seats and turn off all electronic devices. I braced myself for the landing and continued praying until the plane had safely stopped on the gate. When given the green light, we removed our seatbelts and Dayna stood to retrieve our carry-ons from the storage compartment above.

While we waited for our luggage to arrive at baggage claim, Dayna called my brother-in-law to let him know we had landed safely. I scooted near the exit for a breeze of fresh air to call Synatra.

The tall, double-milk chocolate somethin'-somethin' with thick, well-maintained waist-length dreadlocks that was standing in front of me was holding a sign that said 'Jones'. The rays of the sun bounced gently against his hazel-colored eyes. I nearly dropped the phone when Dayna nudged me to bring me back to reality.

After we acknowledged who we were to him, he introduced himself to us as Meego. He must have been a fan of beautiful, thick women because he couldn't keep his eyes off of Dayna and she couldn't resist the temptation to make the best of a flirting situation.

She sashayed her size twenty-two brick house in his direction, rolling her case behind her. He rushed to stop her. "No, no wo-mahn. Let Meego take care uh' dat for you," he commanded in his western Caribbean accent.

"Do what you do then, Mr. Meego!" she retorted batting her eyelashes directly into his gaze.

Our gracious driver held open the door as we got in and then went back around to the driver's side and took off. He opened the sunroof of his self-proclaimed luxury cab and lifted the sounds of some sweet reggae music as he escorted us to The Westin Resort & Casino Aruba. I took in the sights, taking pictures of ducks near the ponds, the trees that swayed, and even the lines in the road. I wanted to capture every moment of this experience.

It really wasn't until we checked into our double-queen, oceanfront executive suite that I was truly able to appreciate the fairytale like charm of paradise. This was a far cry from Myrtle Beach.

The fine, white sandy beaches and rolling blue waters immediately seized my attention. Obediently, I obliged their presence and made my way to the bathroom to get showered and changed. I wasted no time finally planting my curves into a cute little monokini swimsuit I had purchased well over a year ago. I positioned every turn in all the right places, grabbed my beach bag and headed for the door. Dayna, on the other hand, had stretched out across the bed and drifted into a slight slumber just that fast. I left her a note telling her that I would be just in front of the room at the shoreline and to join me once she awakened.

The hotel lobby took on a mind of its own. The décor and the staff reminded me of a scene from a dream I once had. I strolled across the hardwood floor silently dancing in my head. Approaching the row of chaise lounges snuggled against one another between two huge palm trees, I selected the one that yielded the most shade. By the time I placed my towel beneath me the sun had shifted. But, I didn't bother to move. I just wanted to be still and take in the culture in front of me. For this to be a Caribbean island on the other side of the world, there sure were a lot of fine brothers scattered amidst the sands. I'm not really sure what I expected to see but I wasn't expecting all of this walking around me. Must have been some sort of conference or convention or something.

My mind took me to a place of relaxation. The sand tickled my toes while the waters played against my skin. I laid there wondering why I had never retreated to a place like this before. I definitely had to figure out a way to thank my sisters for all of this.

As I took advantage of the daylight, I read a few chapters of my book and after a short while, gathered my things and headed back to the room. I could hear Dayna in the shower so I shouted to let her know that I was back.

"Dee, it's me."

"Quit yelling. I can hear you."

"So, what's on the list for today?"

"Grab the schedule from the side of my iPad bag. I think there is some sort of pool party tonight. Or is it tomorrow night?"

"I have it right here." She was right. The hotel was throwing a stoplight pool party Saturday night. The twist to your traditional pool party was instead of the ladies wearing swimsuits and the men wearing swim trunks, each person was supposed to wear a solid colored t-shirt and shorts. Each color indicated the person's relationship status. Red shirts meant either you were married or in a relationship and you were there to just simply mix and mingle. Yellow shirts meant that there was something going on–but it was complicated. Complications could range from being separated in your relationship or if you were a single married man or woman. If you were single and available, green shirts would be your pleasure, but one had to be careful with this one. The fact that you were wearing green meant that you could be approached by any color and the yellows and greens were always on the prowl. If one color misconstrued what the others' intentions were, you could be in a world of trouble. If you were a tri-sexual, meaning you had a taste for a little of this or a little of that with no strings attached, then blue was your color on the wheel. "Girl, have you read this? What kind of freakiness have you gotten us into?"

"Absolutely nothing. You don't have to go if you don't want to." Just then, Dayna stepped out of the shower and made her way into the bedroom.

"You sound like you are going to go without me if I don't."

"I wouldn't do that. But, please know that I brought my red shirt to let 'em all know I am Mrs. Braylon Malik Walters and there is no other for me. I am happily married, not available, and no longer single. My baby knows he is the onnnnnly onnnnne," she said sounding like Sophia from *The Color Purple*. We high-fived. "It should be fun. If you are not feeling it, then we can come back to the room and just talk and relax."

I continued to read the rest of the schedule to see what other surprises were coming my way. "I'll let you know what's up tomorrow," I advised. The rest of the activities looked inviting, especially the all-white party that was scheduled for tomorrow night. The final goings-on on the schedule revealed that there would be a formal finale which looked just as interesting, so I was glad I brought something fly to wear.

Walking into the living room, Dayna continued to massage the lotion into her hands. "Well, whatever we do, let's make sure we have some fun, even if it means doing absolutely nothing. I'm just happy to be on vacation and with the best sister in the world." We hugged and exchanged a sisterly smile.

"Thanks, Dee. That really means a lot to me. And don't worry. I plan on having some fun. I promise. I will not let you down."

"Good. Now let's go grab a bite to eat."

Chapter 8 - Adrian

For the life of me, I couldn't figure out why I continued to try to watch the revamped *Arsenio Hall Show*. I think some things should just be left alone, because the struggle got real every night.

I set my place setting at the dining room table and finished creating my plate. This kind of living was for the birds. Ever since I could remember, my mother always prepared a hot, home cooked meal and it was times like this that I wish she was here to do the same for me now. I was glad that I was able to learn a few cooking techniques from her because it meant I could feed myself, but there was nothing like a hot meal that a woman poured some love into.

I surfed a few more channels before deciding to watch a re-run episode of *Law & Order*. Just as I settled into the seat at the head of the table there was a knock at the door. I stood quietly and walked over to look out the peephole. There was someone standing on the porch, but I couldn't make out who it was.

I lowered the television volume. "Who is it?"

"It's me." No way. It couldn't be her. Out of all the times I had wished that she would notice me. Just the fact that she was standing on the other side of my door to pay me a visit *outside of work* was all the realization that I needed, but never would I have expected that it would be at this time of night. I quickly ran a number of scenarios to try to figure out what she could possibly want with me. Nothing surfaced. I removed the steel bar from across the door and undid the slide locks.

And there she stood.

She had an hour glass figure that could go on for days. The purple and white halter top shirt snugly lifted her globes to greet me. I gleamed at the curves in her cute little jeans and imagined how she got all of that in them.

"Ms. Jones? What a surprise. What are you doing here?" I looked over her shoulder and on both sides of the building before stopping back at her.

"Adrian, I know it seems strange and real out of order, me just showing up at your spot and all, but I needed to see you about something that couldn't wait."

"What could you possibly have to see me about – at this time of night – that couldn't wait until tomorrow?" I asked her with my Rock eyebrow as confirmation that I was definitely confused.

"Aren't you going to invite me in first?" She leaned back and placed her hand on her hip, waiting for my answer.

I paused for a moment to think about her actions earlier at the restaurant. Through her series of questions, I could see that she was looking at me with a little something more in her eyes than just your typical getting-to-know-you type look. I mean, I had been working there for three years, but this sudden interest in me had me curious. I got the feeling she wanted to know me on another level and her presence here tonight lead me to believe I just may have been right. But, the last thing I needed was something wrong to go down and I get blamed for it just because of my record.

"I'm not so sure about that, Synatra. I mean, it is kind of late."

"Would it make you feel any better if I told you that this visit had nothing to do with work so you can take that 'oh-shit-what-I-do' look up off your face?" I breathed a hard sigh and finally gave in.

"Come in, Ms. Jones." I stepped aside and waved her in.

She looked around my man cave from wall to wall with a look of relief on her face. Sure I once told her about the neighborhood that I lived in when I was hired, but that didn't mean my place was supposed to look like it. The smell of bleach and pine sol was faintly still in the air and I hope it didn't bother her too much. Against the renter's agreement, I had sanded the walls and patched up all of the holes from the previous tenants and completely repainted the place. I replaced all of the hardware on the doors and the kitchen drawers and cabinets. All of the light fixtures were of one design and matched the wood-paneled ceiling fans I had installed in each room. To finish things off, I outfitted the living room with a large corduroy sectional with jumbo accent pillows to suit.

She stepped closer to get a look at my rather unique taste in artwork that adorned each wall in the open living space. The images of creativity continued into the kitchen and dining room, including a one-of-a-kind piece by the late Ernie Barnes.

"Damn. Your shit is tight."

"Thanks, Ms. Jones. Make yourself at home." I grabbed the remote from the arm of the sofa and turned the TV down a bit further. I placed my hands in my pockets and waited on her to drop whatever bombshell she was there to drop. Not wanting to be rude, I offered "Please, have some dinner."

"You love to cook, huh? What you got there?" She peeped around me and looked in the direction of my plate on the table.

"I hooked up some Cajun, garlic shrimp in a lemon cream Alfredo sauce over some fettuccini al dente. I made some homemade parmesan croutons to go with the mixed green salad and a few breadsticks."

"Why you be cookin' like this and you ain't got no woman?" She scanned the view of the room again. My guess was she was looking for pictures or evidence of another woman to confirm her inquiry. "And from the looks of things, you ain't got no kids neither. What's up with that?"

"A man's gotta eat right?" I shrugged my shoulders. "One day, I will have a woman to cook for. But, right now, let me go and fix you a plate because I'm ready to eat." I motioned for her to join me at the table and she complied. As we ate dinner, I learned that there was a little more about her than I thought, and I had to admit it was nice to be in her company without the hustle and bustle of the restaurant business.

She was the youngest of three girls that were but a small piece of her more than two-hundred member family. Her aunts and uncles had a lot of children as did their children and so on. I listened as she told me one of her family stories about the time her grandfather had caught her and this boy from high school in her room fooling around. She thought that he was going to beat the black off of her, but instead her grandfather did something that she wasn't expecting. She figured he left the room to go and get his gun or something, thinking he was going to come back and kill the boy, so she told mister whoever he was to hurry and get dressed and get the hell out of dodge before he came back. Just as dude was about to jump out of the window of their second floor house, in walks her grandfather and hands her a condom and walks out of the room. And get this, it was a magnum! She was all kinds of confused. She was so scared and so nervous, thinking that it was some kind of joke, she told the dude that he had to leave and that she could never see him again. From that point on, she never knew what to expect from her grandfather. It would have been better if he would have just jacked her up and knocked him out cold, but he didn't do any of that and he never mentioned a word about it to her or anyone else as far as she knew.

"Yeah. Sounds to me like your grandfather used some ol' reverse psychology on you!" We laughed as she agreed.

"Yeah, that shit had me all twisted in my damn head. Hell, I'm still scared to be around him for too long because

I be thinkin' he gon' have a flashback or somethin' and choke the shit out of me for disrespecting his house."

"Ms. Jones, can I ask you something?"

"Fa show. What's on your mind?"

"Look, I don't mean any disrespect, but I want to ask you something as Ms. Jones, my evening dinner companion, and not my boss, OK? But, why do you feel the need to curse so much? A lovely young lady such as you doesn't need any of that coming out of her mouth. It taints your beauty." She blushed briefly, but quickly resumed her poker face demeanor.

"You know, I never thought about it. I just be running off at the mouth and they just come flying out all willy-nilly and thangs," She responded as she flapped her hands up in the air. "Does that offend you or somethin'?"

"No. But, I would think that it would offend you."

"Not really, but let's get back to this beauty party."

"Nope. Not until you tell me what you are doing here." This caught her off guard. I waited a moment while she gathered her thoughts.

"I'm here because you never answered my question at the restaurant. What about your family? Do you have any around here?" I hadn't planned on answering that question when she first asked me and I had no intentions on answering it now. Some things were better left unsaid.

"Let me take your plate. Would you like anything else? I made dessert as well." I stood and walked in the kitchen to clear the dishes. Just as I turned to place them in the dishwasher, I bumped into her. She appeared lost in lust as she made her way in front of me, blocking my way.

"Synatra?"

"Adrian?" We engaged in a western stare down.

"Synatra?"

"Adrian?"

"Don't start something you can't finish."

"Oh. I'm not." She took a step closer to me. "I intend to finish it."

"Is that a challenge?" I took a step closer, invading her personal space.

"If it was, are you accepting it?"

I grabbed her hand and kissed the back of it then moved my caress to her palm. "You don't want to get involved with somebody like me. You could get 'a–dickted' and might not want to stop."

"Well, let the high begin." She wrapped her arms around my neck and I did the same to her waist. I gripped her gently and pulled her up, wrapping her legs around my waist. I carried my opponent to my bedroom as my soldier began to rise and prepare for the battlefield.

We kissed impatiently. If I didn't know any better, I would say she had a hint of love behind every smack. Although I had just completed my meal, I was still hungry for the main course.

She slowly undid the buttons on my jeans as I lifted my t-shirt above my head. She began to lick her lips at the sight of my twin towers of power. Seeing that, I made my pecs bounce to tease her desires more.

I reached for her shirt and removed it over her head to find her braless with two plushly, plumped breasts pointed in my direction. She massaged them with her hands and forced them to meet, deepening her cleavage and increasing my yearning. I grabbed her jeans and unhurriedly pulled them down, hovering over her grace land. I raised her legs high above and dropped them on my shoulders. Her back arched as she hissed at the anticipation. Slowly, I began to walk her towards the window, placing her back against the wall. In one swift move, I kneeled before her lunchable and kissed her moistened treat. She winced from the coolness of the partition, but quickly regained her composure the moment I began to lap her cum pocket.

Aggressively, she rammed her body against my face and danced to the rhythm of my tongue. I held her tightly by her waist as she tried to escape her punishment. Just then, I felt her grip tightening on my shoulders and her body began to tense.

Her heightened moment of pleasure caused her to jerk a bit. I had to let her know that I wasn't finished with her so I placed her on the bed on all fours and dared her to move. I let my fingers find her hidden treasure as she whimpered with expectancy. The connection I made with her tunnel of love caused us both to moan in agreement. I stroked her deeply and received them just the same. Each stroke in and out of her was met with her give and take. The arch in her back told me to go deeper and that's just what I did.

"Oh shit!" Her butt bounced off of me like a ripple of water. "Damn. Oh, Synatra!"

"Yes. Don't stop, daddy. Get it."

"I ain't stopping. I ain't stopping." My breathing became much more aggressive and her grunts and wails became increasingly heavier and louder. She reached behind me and pulled me into her as I gripped her shoulders. After much anticipation, we met each other's erotic finale and waited for the intensity of the excitement to lessen.

We looked at each other with moments of satisfaction hanging in the air with neither of us saying a word. After a moment, she reached for her clothes and began to get dressed. I grabbed a pair of gym shorts from my drawer and put them on. As she struggled to stand, I stretched my arm to assist as she wobbled on her feet.

"Well, I guess I'll see you at work tomorrow." She raked her fingers through her hair to regain her feminine composure.

"Indeed. Good night, Ms. Jones." I kissed her on the forehead, led her to the door and walked her to her car. "I thought you had an XF?" I held the door of her ninety-nine Honda Accord open for her.

"I do, but I drive this one when I think I might need to be 'incog-negro'."

"Dang. How many cars do you have?"

"Three." She started the engine and locked it in first gear. "Oh, and by the way, Mr. Cooper. I guess I'm not the only one whose beauty has been tainted. You know, with you and your 'oh shits' and all." I shook my head at her and smiled at her reference to the curse words I'd just used during our session.

"Touché. Get home safely, OK?" I closed the door and watched her drive off down the street and headed back in the house.

Chapter 9 - Synatra

Last night was amazing. I couldn't believe I had the guts to do something like that. *Yes, I could.* Normally, I wouldn't have put myself out there like that, but I took a risk and did something completely outside of myself. *No, I didn't.* He probably thinks I'm some sort of whore, but it's not like that. I tend to go after what I want. Hell, men do it all the time. I'm not saying that I did it just because men do it, but I wanted some sex and I wanted it from him. I am really feeling him, and I have a good feeling about him.

I arrived at the restaurant around six in the morning so that I could have some down time before I started preparing today's dishes. We were running a summer special and because the word was spreading so fast, I had to prepare a little extra than normal.

Upon approach, I noticed the bar lights on and saw Adrian taking inventory of our stock of spirits. I locked the door behind me and took a seat.

"What may I get for you, Miss?" He waited for an answer he already knew. But his attempt at role playing was somewhat of a turn on.

"The usual," I responded.

"Coming right up." He walked around the counter and grabbed my hand, helping me off the bar stool. He pressed his body against mine and gave me a warm hug.

"Thanks, Adrian. I needed that."

"I can tell. You look a bit tense. What's on your mind?"

"Nothing."

"Are you feeling OK after last night?"

"Yep. Couldn't feel better."

"I hope I–we–didn't move too fast. It's not like I want you to think that that is something I do on a regular because I don't."

"Nah. Not at all."

"Is that what you really came for?"

"Yep, and that's not on some hoe type shit either."

"Not at all. We're both adults and we made an adult decision together. That's all." He squeezed me tighter. "Do you need anything else?"

"Yeah. I need some more of you," I flirted, "but first I'm going to go in here and start prepping this food."

"You can have some more of me anytime. And, I do mean anytime." He lifted my chin and kissed me softly on the lips.

"Is that right?" He leaned me against the bar and rammed his sweet tongue down my throat. He palmed his hand over my breast. As I participated, I rubbed the back of his neck letting my hand travel down his strong, brawny back and grip his tight, muscular ass real good. He hurriedly removed my hands and stepped back.

"You can touch me anywhere but there." I kissed him and smiled.

"Baby, I would love to keep the show moving, but I need to get to work."

"Yeah, and I need to finish this inventory check." He kissed my forehead and graced his finger alongside my cheek. "You are so ravishing. I appreciate your unique kind of beautiful. Thank you."

"Thanks, but thank you for what?"

"Can a man just say thank you without there being some underlying reason?"

"Hell naw, not to me. I need to know what's on your mind. What's up?"

"We'll talk about it later."

"Well, all I know is you just told me thank you and I haven't done anything." He didn't respond. I moved around him and walked towards the back, leaving him standing with a tent in his pants. "But, I know one thing. The eyes don't lie and your eyes are saying a whole lot." I stepped into the kitchen and let the door swing back and forth behind me.

Chapter 10 - Chance

Morgan and I went to the hotel bar and chopped it up like we used to do back in the day. We talked about old college stories and how well our careers were going.

One story he brought up that I had completely forgotten about was the time when he discovered that the snack machine in the basement of the dorm wasn't locked.

He had gone down to the laundry room to retrieve a load of fresh towels from the dryer when he heard a slight tapping noise coming from the canteen area. Normally, black people are the last ones to go looking for strange sounds, but that fool did. And when he did, he discovered that the door to the snack machine was not closed all the way. The next thing you know, he began to raid machine and stuffed them in his laundry basket. He tried to arrange the towels to conceal them, but I'm not so sure he was fooling anybody but himself.

I headed that way to see what was taking him so long and met him in the hallway. We went back to his room and you would have thought we hit the lottery. We had cookies, cakes and chips for days. And don't let some of the fellas with the munchies come around because we started selling them for a dollar to two dollars apiece.

We laughed about the memory and reminisced more about life on the yard.

I flipped through his wallet to check out the latest family pictures he was carrying. The smile on his face when he talked about his family secretly had me wishing I had a family of my own. I never shared with him any of my familial desires, but I was sure he knew. The way my face would light up when he updated me on the happenings in his life was a dead giveaway if you asked me. But, that type of thing never happened for me. Right after college, I immediately enrolled in the MBA program at Wake Forest University, completing the program in less than two years. I was just that focused. I felt like if I completed it sooner than expected, I would be in a prime position to earn a decent wage to prepare for a family, but that didn't happen either.

Through all of the sacrifice I had made to advance my education, life had somehow managed to keep going while I was left standing with three degrees, numerous professional certifications, three cars, a four-thousand square-foot home that boasts a five-car garage, five bedrooms and six bathrooms. But, there was only one thing missing – the most important in my opinion – a wife.

My life had been led by nothing but Christ and because of that I'd never been the type of brother to date just anybody. I simply could not share my fortunes, dreams or my "jewels" with every female that claimed she was the right woman for me. I had dated a little bit here and there, but no one seemed to match my ability to seek a virtuous woman instead of a virtual woman, the kind that was made up to be anything she had to be to get what she wanted. Besides, I preferred quality over quantity any day. I decided to obey Him and wait for the woman He sent for me and not a moment sooner would I attempt to wife up just any ol' woman. No, she had to have been made just for me.

"Dang, man. Look at her. She's getting big." My goddaughter, Malendria, was already in kindergarten, or in 'big people school' as she liked to call it.

"Yeah, man. They grow up fast, real fast, but I wouldn't change it for anything in the world."

"How is Mevelyn doing?"

"She's doing good man. Real good." He took a sip of water.

"That's what's up." Mevelyn hadn't been feeling up to her usual self the last time I talked to Morgan. The last thing he told me was that she was constantly experiencing headaches and was always nauseous. "Well, look here man. We've got a busy schedule tomorrow so I'ma go back upstairs and look over the materials one last time. You straight?

"Yeah, I'm good. I'll be there to support you with the literature distribution and collecting the evaluation forms."

We dapped each other up and I headed back to the elevator bay. He headed for the restaurant.

By the time I got back upstairs, I found that I could hardly hold a thought in my head or concentrate. I was pretty confident in the materials I was scheduled to present in the morning so there was no need to overdo it. I figured I may as well head back downstairs and check out the scene. Maybe Morgan was still in the restaurant and I could meet back up with him, I thought.

The evening hostess greeted me as I approached the stand.

"Good evening, sir. Just one?"

"Yes. Just one, but I'm looking for someone. He's about five-ten, medium build, wears glasses?"

"Oh, yes, Mr. Brooks. He just left a few minutes ago. He's such a jokester!"

"Yes. He is a character, isn't he?" I scanned the area one last time. "But, I guess I could stay and have a drink or two."

"Right this way, sir." She led me to a small, private oceanfront table that was clearly meant for two. "Someone will be with you in just a moment, sir"

After a few minutes, a young, Caribbean lady sashayed her way towards me.

"Evening, sir. What might I get for you this evening?"

"Just an iced tea with lemon for now."

"Sure thing. Coming right up."

CNN was showing a few of the latest news updates from around the world. Of them, it was reported that a high school football championship game had been canceled due to some sort of fight between the opposing football coaches of two schools. The story had to have been huge if it made national news this quickly.

I would be willing to bet anybody that every attorney that could practice law in South Carolina was all over this one. From the outside looking in and based on the news report, this type of thing had the potential to make some heads roll. The ripple effect from the legalities surrounding this cloud of accusations could prove extremely costly to whomever – or whichever school – was at fault. From the money that was lost from the city investments and the surrounding areas, to the ticket sales that were reverted because the game was canceled. This thing had the potential to be huge. I don't even want to think about all of the parents, friends, alumni and local supporters that were planning to attend the game and had made travel arrangements. Have you seen the cost to change an airline itinerary? Local screen printers were probably due to lose some revenue as well as I am sure each school had probably pre-ordered their championship attire.

My drink was delivered along with a basket of chips. I snacked on a few as I continued to watch the news broadcast. Finishing both, I left a twenty to cover the bill and decided once again to head back to the room.

While I waited for one of the elevators to return to the lobby floor, I grabbed one of the free real estate guides and reviewed the outside cover. I was always interested in what the market looked like in different parts of the world.

Just then the elevator dinged, signaling the arrival of my chariot. The doors opened and outstepped two of the most beautiful women I had ever laid eyes on. One of them especially caught my attention. I found myself unable to move my feet as I waited for them to exit the elevator. They were obviously laughing and giggling about something.

"Evening, ladies."

"Good evening" they said in unison.

My eyes followed them across the lobby as I merged the one on the left into my tunnel vision. Her hair swayed loosely across her back as her hips see-sawed with each step. I recognized the fragrance she left behind to keep me company in the elevator once I was finally able to step inside. I pressed the button for the fifteenth floor and waited patiently for my arrival.

I made my way to the bedroom and showered until I felt I had completely washed the day away. My mind was still swirling around that lovely lady that tickled my imagination at the elevator bay. I hadn't had the courage to ask her for her name. I couldn't even move my feet let alone talk. I simply hoped that I would be able to see her again during my stay so I said a small prayer that they weren't headed to check out of the hotel.

***

The grand ballroom was filled with the bruhs of Phi Alpha Phi from all over the world. Everyone was abuzz to find out the latest happenings in each other's lives, talking about careers, education, family and of course the football championship game heard around the world. This was the perfect time to meet and network with one another.

Having been identified as the number one non-profit organization for seven years straight and were ranked number one for scholarship and service for just as long, it was no wonder that our membership had grown more than eighty percent.

The meeting was called to order and every one took their seats. Each director introduced himself as the audience applauded each region. I was the last presenter so I provided the technical assistance with each presentation.

One after another, each member shared some of the latest research that was being conducted in their group. Topics ranged from generational educational gaps in African-Americans to working with adult learners in the community college system. By the time it was time for me to present, Morgan had gotten into place to distribute hard copies of the presentation and copies of the evaluation form.

They responded just as I knew they would. At the end, we spent nearly another hour answering questions about the proposal placed before them. A lot of the bruhs were interested in bringing this type of program back to their regions. Some of them had already sent emails and text messages to local school superintendents and to a few freshmen orientation coordinators for numerous institutions of higher learning. For the most part, I think we were on to something that had the potential to change the lives of many young minority males. If we could tap into this group and help to change their lives for the better the world would become a better place because of it.

After seven long hours of meals and presentations, we wrapped up the session and hung around to answer any last minute questions anyone may have had. I noticed Morgan speaking with a group from the west coast. They were laughing and joking around. No doubt that he had said or done something that had them all holding their sides from laughing too hard.

I finished packing the rest of my things and signaled to Morgan that I was heading out. He acknowledged and kept on doing his drunken man version of the strike step routine.

The lobby was full of members, too. So much so that some of the new check-ins had to maneuver around them to get to the front counter. The elevator came just as I approached so I joined a group of members from the midwest on the ride up. No doubt I used the opportunity to exchange a few cards and social media information bits. After stopping on floors six and thirteen, I reached for my key card to prepare for my exit.

I could tell that the housekeeping staff had been to the room to clean because the curtains had been left open. The nighttime view from the room was amazing. I hurried and changed out of my suit and hard bottoms and into my linen pant suit to prepare for the white party tonight. After a quick shower and shave, I made my way back downstairs to the party site.

Chapter 11 - Dayna

A sea of black men surrounded us as we waded through the lobby. Light-skinned, brown-skinned, dark-skinned, midnight. They all looked beautiful. There was something about a man, especially a black man, in a suit. We eased through the crowd as best as we could and finally made our way to the taxi stand.

"Vay, let's walk instead so we can take some time to see the island after we finish eating."

"Sounds good to me. Where to?"

We headed towards one of the adjacent hotels as there appeared to be a row of shops and restaurants in that direction when we came upon a small bistro-style restaurant. The display case had some of the freshest looking meats I had ever seen. We glanced at the menu, placed our order and found a table next to the stage area. A reggae band was still setting up so we decided to chill for a bit to hear the sounds of some authentic reggae music.

Our food arrived just as my stomach began to growl for the one-hundredth time. I ordered the BBQ rubbed smoked salmon with a sweet and spicy chili sauce and Vay ordered a mixed green salad topped with grilled jerk chicken and a homemade blueberry vinaigrette dressing. The food looked delicious and smelled just the same. With the opportunity to eat all we could stand, I would have to make sure we came back so that we could try out their breakfast.

After Vay blessed the food and the hands that had prepared it, we dug in. Neither one of us said anything for about five minutes; the food was just that good.

"So, this is what it's like to have some authentic Caribbean food, huh?" Vay said after stuffing her mouth with a forkful of salad.

"Yes, big sis. So enough about that rabbit food you're eating. I know you saw that fine, tall drink of water staring you down at the elevator today."

"What are you talking about?"

"Vay, don't play with me. You know good and darn well that you saw that man see you and don't think I didn't see *you* smile from ear to ear when we walked past him. Why you trying to act like you don't know what I'm talking about?" She continued eating her food, totally ignoring my comments. "Look, Vay. I know what you've been through, OK. I know you have many scars. But, you have to get back out there. Take a chance. You are so beautiful, so talented and smart. You would make any man a perfect wife and any child a perfect mother. Don't you agree?"

She continued eating.

"Vay? Vay? I know you hear me."

"What do you want me to say? Yes, I saw him, OK. How could I not? That is the first man that has looked at me like that in I don't know how many years. So, yes. I noticed him."

"I really wish you could see what I see." She ignored yet another comment and continued eating. "So are you going to talk to him?"

"What?"

"Are you going to talk to him?"

"How do you know that he even wants to talk to me? All he did was look at me."

"It's not *that* he looked at you, it's *how* he looked at you." I said pointing my fork in her direction. "Don't play dumb. And, I'm telling you now. If that man approaches you, you better give him your attention." She laughed and we continued eating.

A loud bang on the cymbal got our attention as the lead singer crept up on the mic. The reggae vibes grooved mightily throughout the pub. One couple got up to dance when another couple joined them. We sat back and chilled for a bit, just taking in the sounds.

I thought about my Braylon and what he might be up to. I couldn't wait to get home and love on him. This would be the longest time I have been away from him since we've been married. I am sure he understood the need to be with my sister at this time. He helped me and Synatra plan for this getaway so I know he didn't mind my being gone.

Looking at the two couples dance in the middle of the floor had me longing for his touch. What I wouldn't give to have my man's hands all over me. Six more days and I would know just what I was missing. Maybe when Vay gets in the shower I will call him and we can Facetime because Lord knows I missed my husband and I was sure he felt the same.

"Let's get ready to head back. I want to make sure I have enough time to get ready for tonight." Nevaeh glanced at the bill on the table and reached for her purse.

"That's OK. I got it. It's on me."

"You sure, girl?"

"Yeah. This is your week. Let me take care of everything." I tipped our server a ten and we scooted away from the table. We put a little pep in our step as we headed out and walked towards the shopping center.

Chapter 12 - Nevaeh

Dayna was right. I knew from the moment we stepped off that elevator that that tall, fine gentleman that spoke to us was like a dream come true. He reminded me of a mocha-caramel dipped Idris Elba. His scent played with my emotions as I walked past him. I was definitely sure to put a little extra umph in my stride. I figured if he was going to look then I may as well give him something to look at.

We got back to the hotel and there were still a few men gathered around one of the enormous planters near the cascading water fall posing for a group photo.

As I stepped out of the shower and made my way towards the living room, I noticed Dayna lying across the bed with a huge grin on her face. I waited for her to get in before I pulled out my "go-go-get'em-girl" dress. I sat at the vanity in the bathroom and carefully made up my face making sure to achieve a flawless look but without too much product. The flat irons were almost at a durable temperature so I prepped my hair and waited. Still, nothing was on the TV, so I moved to the outdoor terrace and took in the night air.

From the looks of things, a good little crowd had already begun to gather on the beach. A steel drum band was rumbling near the pier and the beach butlers were making their rounds.

"What you doing, chick?"

"Checking out the scene."

"What's it looking like?"

"Like a chocolate fountain!" We both laughed and I stepped back inside.

I touched up my hair and ran the flat iron through Dayna's hair as well. I did one more check on my make-up and we headed for the door.

"Dayna, do me a favor?"

"What's that?"

"Promise me you won't leave me by myself. I know how you like to dance and all and you liable to leave me hanging."

"Girl, come on here. Let's go and have a good time!"

The weather was perfect for tonight's party. The scene was filled with pure white everything all across the beachfront. Curtains of white string lights cascaded down the sides of the bar area. The outdoor uplights added a nice elegant touch to the ambiance.

The bar was crowded with partygoers looking to get their fair share of the complimentary liquid courage. I carefully made my way through the crowd and ordered a cranberry and pineapple juice spritzer for me and an amaretto sour for Dayna. I bobbed my head and tapped the bar to the old school beat of 'Rock the Bells'. The DJ was nice.

Just when I received our drinks and turned to pass one to Dayna, somebody bumped into me, spilling my drink all over my dress. It was ruined. I regained my posture and shook my head at the stain that was quickly setting in.

"Oh, no. Miss. I am so sorry." I looked up and saw that it was him. The 'him' that caught my eye at the elevator. The 'him' that burned a hole into my backside as he watched me walk away. The 'him' that was standing before me. He was grabbing napkin after napkin from the dispenser on the countertop.

"It's quite alright." I stood with my arms agape, marveling at the masterpiece that had been created on my person by this strange artist.

"No, no. It's not alright. Please, tell me your name."

Not one for wanting to reveal my identity to some foreigner, I said, "Puddin' Tang."

He laughed and so did I. His smile was snow white. The shallow dimples that appeared on his face called for my attention even further.

"Well, Miss 'Puddin' Tang', as if that is your real name, my name is Chance but my friends call me Prez." He extended his hand to shake mine and I returned the gesture.

"Well, what shall I call you?"

"I hope, in time, you will call me your husband, but I'll settle with Prez for now," he said, still holding onto my hand. "Let me take care of this for you. Send me your dry cleaning bill, OK. I'm in room number –

"It's OK. Really, it is." I grabbed a napkin from his free hand and began to blot the spot on the front of my dress.

"May I at least get you another drink?"

"Do you think you can do that with just one hand?" He realized that he was still holding mine and quickly let it go. "Thanks, but, no, thank you. I really should get changed out of this dress and start a soak." Just then, Dayna moved closer to me.

"Vay, you alright, girl?" She looked me up and down at the mess that was made.

"Yes. I'm fine."

"Well, if I was in the company of a nice looking man like this I would be fine, too." She smirked at him and winked at me. I gave her the side eye. "And, to whom do I have the pleasure of being acquainted?" She put on her rendition of a fancy dignitary and flapped her hand as if to wave him off.

"Dayna, this is Chance. Chance this is my sister, Dayna."

"Nice to meet you, Dayna," he greeted.

"Likewise, romance, I mean, Chance." I gave her another side eye, this time with a little more attitude than the last.

"Hey, listen. I'm going to head back to the room to take care of this."

"But, naw, for real. What happened?" She still looked horrified at the stain on my dress.

"Well, this kind gentleman sort of bumped into me and spilled my drink all over me."

"Now, that's what I'm talking about! A brother been on the scene two minutes and already trying to get you out – she emphasized – of that dress and *in* to his bed! Way to go Chance!" He blushed. She raised her hand in a high five position like some crazed fan waiting on him to celebrate a Panthers touchdown with her.

"OK. Well, I'll go with you." Dayna took another sip of her drink in attempt to hurry and finish it.

"No. Dee. You stay here. I'll be fine."

"Nope. You know the rule. We come together, we leave together, no matter what."

"Fine." I spun around to place the empty glass on the bar.

"Please, ladies. Allow me to escort you to your room; that's the least I could do. This way, please." Chance held his guiding hand and directed us towards the lobby area and even further back to the loading area.

The ride up to the twelfth floor was somewhat awkward. I managed to not buckle from the pressure of having this fine specimen of a man stand behind me and Dayna managed to not control her grimacing and smirking the whole ride up.

He quietly stood at the back of the elevator, as we approached our floor.

"Well, this is us. Thank you again for the escort."

"My pleasure. Here, let me get that for you." He stepped around us to hold the door open. "So, Vay, for how long are you and your sister on the island?" He smiled at the victory of calling me by the name he had heard Dayna say.

Dayna walked ahead of us, fumbling to find the key card as she made her way towards the room.

"We'll be here for the rest of the week. And you?" We continued to walk slowly in the same direction.

"The same. I'm here for the Phi Alpha Phi Convention."

"Oh, that's nice. We're just here on a sister-to-sister vacation."

"Vay, may I ask you something?"

"You may."

"Would it be OK if I took you out to dinner tomorrow night?"

"It's OK. She doesn't mind!" Dayna's nosey tale had been eavesdropping all the way down the hall. He laughed and I tried to hold back a look of embarrassment from my face.

"Well, do you mind?"

"No, I don't mind. Not at all." I stopped in front of room 1212. "Well, this is me. Thanks again for everything."

"The pleasure is all mine, Vay."

"Well, I will see you around then."

"I hope so." He turned and headed back down the hall way and I entered the room and locked the door. Dayna was waiting on the couch wearing a Chester cheese smile on her face.

"So, what did he say?"

"Nothing. He wants to take me to dinner, as if you didn't already know that." I leaned back so Dayna could unzip my dress and let it fall to the floor. I prepared a warm soak in the bathroom sink and submerged the dress.

THE SIDE EFFECTS OF LOVE

"Surely, you told him 'yes'?"

"I did." Dayna screamed and jumped up on the couch. "Oh, girl. Sit down!"

We talked into the wee hours of the morning after ordering room service and having a few more drinks. Soon after, sleep found us in the living room with Dayna on the couch and me on the chaise.

Chapter 13 - Nia

Thanks to Dr. Mathis I had at least half a day left to enjoy. I can't remember the last time I had gotten off work early, but I was sure to make the best of it.

I checked my phone to see if I had any messages. I noticed two missed text messages from my girl, Synatra. The first message said she needed to talk. The second message screamed code blue as she sent 'EMERGENCY' in all caps. I dialed her number and waited for it to connect before I pulled away from the office. She answered on the fourth ring.

"What up, cow?"

"Hey, Synatra. What it do?"

"I can't call it. Same shit, different toilet."

"Girl, you crazy. What you up to?"

"Nothing. Just wanted to holler at my girl real quick. Hadn't heard from you in a minute so I thought I would get at you."

"Uh oh. What's wrong?"

"Why something gotta be wrong?"

"'Cause I've known you since the third grade, Synatra. I know you. Besides, you text me 'EMERGENCY'" The underlying sound in her voice told me that something was definitely wrong. Never had she contacted me just to see what was up. The funny thing about it was we could go months without talking, for one reason or another, but we would always pick up right where we left off as if we hadn't missed a beat.

She continued making small talk and I continued to listen, waiting for that moment when the flood gates would open and her true intentions would come pouring out.

"So, what time do you get off work?"

"I'm already off. My boss man gave me a half-day so I just left the office."

"That's what's up."

"Stop stalling, Syn', and holla' at cha girl."

"OK. Look, I need to talk to you, Nia. I've been having a hard time dealing with something and I don't quite know how to handle it."

"What do you mean?"

"Girl, come to the spot and let me treat you to lunch. This ain't the kind of conversation I really want to have over the phone, ya dig?"

"No problem. I'll be there in just a bit."

"Cool. See you when you get here."

I pulled into the EpiCentre parking deck and parked next to Synatra's car in one of the reserved spots marked for the restaurant. I set my phone to vibrate so that our conversation wouldn't be interrupted and headed for the front doors.

The lunch crowd had already filled the place by the time I arrived. No sooner than I walked in the hostess summoned me to follow her.

"Right this way, Ms. Arnold."

"How did you know my name?"

"Oh, I make it a habit to know all of our customers. Besides, Ms. Jones pointed you out already."

She led me to the rear of the business and directly to a large conference room. The room was tastefully decorated with an exquisite cherry wood, oval meeting table. The plant columns that adorned the corners of the room each hosted a jumbo fern. The overhead lighting cast a glow of serenity. I hung my coat in the armoire and took a seat at one of the place settings. Before I got too comfortable, Synatra entered the room.

"There she is!"

"'Sup girl?" We hugged each other and rocked from side to side.

"Nothing much. Thank you for agreeing to meet me for lunch." She pressed an intercom button and requested a server to come to the conference room. After placing our orders we engaged in small chit chat until our food was delivered. She invited me to bless the food and afterwards we began to eat.

"Look. I know you are wondering what in the world I wanted to talk about that couldn't be said over the phone."

"I'm listening."

"Here goes – I'm about to do something that is totally outside of the box. You know ol' boy that I promoted to manager?"

"The one that started out as a cook? The ex-convict?"

"Yeah, that's the one."

"What about him?" I looked at her impatiently waiting for an answer. "Don't tell me you about to do what I think you're about to do?"

"You damn right. I gotta have him, girl."

"From the looks of things – the way you are grinning and all – I would say you have already had him."

Shamefully, she admitted, "And, you would be right." I shook my head waiting for the details of what was sure to come after this admission. "The thing is, as many dudes as I have been in contact with, he is the only one that I truly feel a decent connection with. Truth be told, when it went down between us, I'm not so sure that he even wanted to go there with me, but he did."

"So, when did all of this happen?"

"A few nights ago, at his spot. I only went there to chill with him, as a friend you know because I wanted to find out more about the question that he failed to answer, but then things took a different turn and the next thing you know he pinned me against the damn wall!"

"Nah! You went there with all intentions of sexing that man up. I know you, girl!" We laughed. "Did you at least use protection?" She shook her head. "No? Are you serious?"

"Girl, we ain't have time to get no papa stopper. I know I should have, but I didn't even think about it. I was ripe and ready, you heard me? And, he was, too!"

"OMG, Syn! I can't believe you took it there?"

"OK. Damn! I took it there. I really didn't mean to. Honest!" *At least my toes were crossed.*

"You know this jeopardizes things don't you?"

"What 'chu mean?"

"Syn', he's your employee. I mean, this man works for you. Not to mention he is an ex-convict that you hired," I said as I picked up my pickle on the side. "What were you thinking and why were you thinking it?"

"Look, all I know is that I saw something that I wanted and damn-it I went for it. The overwhelming connection that I felt between us just couldn't go unnoticed."

"But, why all of a sudden now? I mean, he's worked for you for about three years, right?"

"Yep – it's been three years. I was the one trying to hold it in. I mean sure, I noticed him checking me out several times, but my guess was that he didn't want to take it there because he worked for me and he was just trying to keep his head down, you know. I checked his background and aside from this one serious bid he did he came up clean."

"So what are you going to do now that you've already given your cookies to this monster?"

"Don't say that!" I saw that she was noticeably offended by my last comment so I decided to withdraw it.

"Sorry. My bad." She held her head down as if she was thinking about her reaction, too. "Well, has he said anything about it since it happened?"

"Umm, we kind of talked about it but not in so many words."

"I don't understand."

"Well, we busted a slob on one another and he said he was cool. Then, later he told me that he wanted to talk to me about something and asked me out to dinner."

"What did you say?"

"I said 'yes'. We're supposed to hook up tonight. Taryn is gon' hold things down for us while we're out."

"Do you think he is feeling some type of way about what went down?"

"Not really. I don't know what it is, but if he is, then I would just have to back off and treat him like the subordinate he is."

"Girl, you crazy!"

"I'm just saying. I'm still the Queen B up in here." She shoved a finger into her chest while rocking her head from side to side.

The conference room door opened and we both turned to see who had entered.

It was Adrian.

We looked at each other, I'm sure wondering the same thing – how much of the conversation had he heard?

He stopped midway into the room when he noticed us sitting at the table. "Hey, ladies. Please pardon my interruption. I didn't know anyone was in here."

"No problem, Mr. Cooper." I looked back and forth between him and Synatra to see if I could see any signs that he heard what was said.

"'Sup, Mr. Cooper?"

"Ms. Jones." He placed his hands behind his back and started to walk back out.

Synatra stopped him as he reached for the door. "Did you need me for anything?"

"Not at all, Ms. Jones. I was going to use the room to have my lunch and work on some new information."

"What new information?" Synatra raised her eyebrows in total shock. I sat quietly and watched the scene play out.

"The new information that I planned to share with you at our team meeting on Thursday." He waited as she absorbed the news as he nodded and grinned.

"Oh, Ah-ight. I guess I'll haf'ta wait 'til then to see what's up, huh?"

"I should hope so, Ms. Jones. I am sure that you will be most pleased with the outcome." With that, he slowly turned and removed himself from the room.

I shook my head and laughed at the moment. Noticing this, Synatra just looked at me, waiting for me to comment either way.

"What?" Synatra leaned back further into her chair.

"What, what?" I hunched my shoulders clearly playing boo-boo the fool.

"Don't what me, Nia! What's on your mind? Speak on it."

"Nothing at all, but if you want me to say that I would have been able to tell that something was up between you two even if you wouldn't have told me then I would be lying to you and I don't want to do that."

"How so?"

"First of all, as if the mile-long smile on your face wasn't enough, he looked at you with a look of pleasure."

"You saw all of that within the two seconds he was in here?"

"Umm hmmm." Synatra dropped her head and played with her salad a bit. "Look, all I'm saying is this – if you think this is the road that you are able to travel and not get caught up then I'm all for it. Just be careful 'cause you know how you can get."

"And how is that?"

"You sometimes sabotage things and can sometimes come off as an above-it-all type chick." She leaned forward at this revelation. "I'm just saying. You can sometimes act like you 'got this', like you got to where you are by yourself and that you don't need anybody in the world. You can get in your own way sometimes. But, on the real, everybody needs somebody, Syn, and if you are serious about this thing with him, don't play with that man's heart and don't push him away if you start developing some serious feelings for him."

"What you mean 'I act like I don't need anybody in the world?"

"Remember Hendrix?" She crossed her legs and folded her arms across her chest clearly feeling some type of way about that friendly reminder.

Hendrix was a guy she had dated back when we were in our early twenties. He came from an affluent background with nothing but the world at his beck and call. But, for some reason, he was always fascinated with the 'hood life. Both his parents were lawyers and so were his maternal grandparents.

His father's people hailed from a long line of educators and entrepreneurs of various areas of interests. But, somehow Hendrix always found himself on the East side every weekend. He really believed that he grew up in that life and that the hood was where he belonged. And, then he met Synatra. Once she found out that he came from money, that poor girl used him for everything he was worth. She even went so far as to tell him that she was pregnant with twins and that it could cost fifteen hundred dollars to abort both babies at an exclusive clinic in Raleigh. And, he believed her.

The next day one of his boys spotted her at the mall balling and captured a clip of her on his cell phone laughing and smiling all up in some other dude's face. When Hendrix saw it he was devastated. After circling the parking lot and finding her car – the one he had put in his name and given her money for the down payment - he parked a few rows away outside one of the restaurant entrances at the mall and waited for her to come out. Just like he had watched when the video was sent to him, sure enough, she was trying to hold her cell phone on her shoulder while she juggled bags upon bags on her arms in search of her car key. He watched as the dude she was in the video clip with caught up to her and helped her with them. After seeing them exchange a few kisses, he calmly walked over to where they were both standing. Just then, a couple of Charlotte's finest showed up on the scene. Hendrix had reported the car stolen and they were there to arrest her. After issuing her a citation for unauthorized use of conveyance, they hit her with a five hundred dollar fine with a scheduled court date in three weeks. She cussed him out real good and thought she could get away with telling him that her "new man" she had just met would take care of everything. When that coward dropped her bags and ran back to the entrance to catch the number eighteen bus, she was left stranded with the dumbest look on her face.

The charges were eventually dropped because the judge ruled that since they were a couple and the car was in his name, he had given her the keys to the car so technically it wasn't stolen. She had had the car for more than six months when he reported it stolen so the grand theft auto charge was thrown out. That poor guy never spoke to her again. Instead, he started dating her former best friend and neighbor, Balenda. The last I heard, they were together for about a year before he finally woke up and realized that she was only with him for his money, too.

"All I'm saying is I hope you have moved past that stinking thinking and that you have emotionally matured."

"Thanks for the reminder, but I hear you, Nia. I hear you. You don't have to worry about that. I am past all that and I wouldn't do that to Adrian. He, unlike all of the others, is a really nice guy and if this thing works out I want to do nothing but right by him, ya dig?"

"Sure thing." I lifted my sandwich to get another bite. "Now, let's finish this lunch so you can get back to work."

She playfully threw a pack of salad crackers at me. "I see you got jokes!"

"Yep, sure do! I think I may go to the store and pick up something to cook tonight."

"Well, thanks for joining me for lunch. Be sure to keep in touch."

"And you do the same."

Chapter 14 - Braylon

I was happy to hear from my baby this morning and was even more thankful that I was fully awake when she called. I was already running a little behind, but speaking with her was well worth the delay.

When I spoke to her, I purposely didn't tell Dayna about the lawsuit pending against her because I wanted her and Vay to have a good time on their trip. The news of such a travesty would have been devastating to her. I decided it was best for me to handle things for her until she returned to the states.

I checked my watch, realizing that I needed to place a call to the office to let Justin and Kennedy know that I would be in a little later. Erin, our legal assistant, had already emailed me a copy of the documents I would need for my review and Kalindra had researched and provided a list of professional resources we would need when we went to trial.

That girl could do some research. We would need the best medical experts in the field if we had a chance at winning our case and because of her ability to think completely outside of the box, she had managed to find a few medical experts that would set the perfect tone for the defense we were preparing to present.

According to my schedule, I was only committed to two meetings today. Thankfully, they were early morning gatherings so that would leave me enough time for lunch and provide me with an opportunity to run by the shop to let Jessica know what was going on.

I jumped in the car and dialed the office. Erin answered on the first ring and transferred me to Kennedy.

"Kennedy? What's going on, man?"

"Another day, another dollar."

"I heard that. Well, I hope you can hear me OK. I've got you connected through the Bluetooth."

"Oh, I can hear you just fine. I take it this call is about Dayna's case, right?"

A month before Dayna and Vay left for their sisters vacation, I received an urgent message at the office. As was reported to me by Kalindra, Dayna was being sued by a frequent visitor to the bakery. Franklin Austin, the plaintiff's husband had filed the suit because they claimed that because Dayna's muffins, pastries and more specifically her key lime crème cupcakes, were too delicious, and that they were the cause of her weight gain and the reason she developed type II diabetes. She further claimed that the ingredients used contained a chemical that was highly addictive and that the sugar she used contained fifty percent more sucralose and was not regulated by the food and drug administration.

Dayna was being sued for twenty-five million dollars.

A certified notice was delivered the same day that told us that the wife was in the hospital and was currently in a diabetic coma.

Through all of the hard work and sacrifice Dayna made, I knew this was sure to devastate her. Not once had she been sued. In fact, business was beginning to pick up. She had recently secured a partnership with the Carolina Panthers to serve as their confectionary caterer for all of the club level box suites and for any pre-game hospitality events they held. As a way to give back to the community, in conjunction with the Panthers deal, she gave away free cupcakes to the first five hundred visitors that came to the fan zone before every home game. Each week featured a different flavor and the fans loved it. They proved it by increasing her business by more than forty percent.

Now that this Mrs. Sadie Austin was in the hospital, we had to delay the trial slightly to allow enough time for her to recover. Hence, we would use the time to strengthen our defense against the Austins.

"Absolutely. I think we've got this one in the bag."

"Good. Good. That's great to hear. So, tell me, what are our chances? I mean, I know my position on this, but I want to make sure that we have searched every crevice of the law on this one. This could have the potential to create some unnecessary stress and I want to be proactive as such."

"Yes, sir. I understand. I'll get Kalindra right on it and I will personally make sure that we are in a prime position to reach a victory in this case."

"Thanks. Would you connect me with Justin, please?"

"Certainly."

Justin and I spoke for the remainder of my ride to the office. The traffic was beginning to pick up on Interstate 77 so I was sure to engage our conversation further as it related to the list of witnesses and demonstrative evidence we were preparing.

Seeing the exit nearing uptown, I decided to take a detour and stop by the shop to pick up some pastries to take to the office.

"Hey, Justin. Let everyone know that I'm bringing in some breakfast goodies so we may want to go ahead and get some coffee brewing. It's going to be a long day." I checked my mirrors one last time, signaled and exited the freeway. "See y'all in a bit."

ˈParking was non-existent as usual so I made my way to the executive parking garage and filled one of the bakeries reserved spaces. My phone had vibrated several times during my call, so I began to check messages as I walked towards the store. The sounds of the city were already beginning to fill the air. Some of the local musicians were playing buckets or bass guitars to offer the public a feeling of easement as one after another made their way into their respective destination.

By the time I had reached the third text message, the sticky bun fragrant was fluttering through the air. I followed my nose to the entrance of the bakery just as one of the downtown couriers was making her way out with an armful of orders.

"Braylon Walters!" By the time I had turned around to see who had called me, a shot gun blast gauged me in the chest and pinned me against the building. The weight from my body stiffened and I began fall down.

Chapter 15 - Chance

The alarm screamed at me to wake up. I could barely open my eyes let alone hit the snooze button to catch a few more Z's. With my eyes still closed, I reached for the remote and scanned a few channels until I heard the news.

I threw on a t-shirt and some shorts and made sure my shoes were properly laced and headed for the fitness center. I had missed my work out for the past two days; I couldn't go without a third day.

By the time I reached mile five on the treadmill, I was beginning to feel as if I had caught my second wind. I jumped off long enough to grab a fresh towel to keep the sweat from running into my eyes. Just as I wiped the corner of my right eye, I looked up and saw that amazing black beauty that I bumped into last night. From the looks of things, she was in her cool down phase from a long run. The way she checked her Fitbit and jogged in place told me so. I watched her swipe her cell phone and stretch a few muscles. The way she bent left to right and then dropped into a full squat to stretch her inner thighs had me staring a hole into her.

She made her way to the side entrance so I hurried to open it from the inside. We locked eyes. She smiled. "We meet again." She held up a finger, signaling for me to wait as she removed her earbuds.

"Hey, there!"

"Hello, again!" I extended my hand and she received it. "How was the run?"

"Great! Whoo – that's just what I needed!" Her breathing steadied as she removed her cell phone armband.

"Do you work out often?"

"When I can. I really need to put forth more effort, though. I gotta keep it tight, ya know?"

"Looks just fine to me." I unconsciously sized her up being careful to pause briefly at the curves that surrounded her frame. She hesitated then revealed a shy grin. A bit embarrassed I said, "Please forgive me. I hope I wasn't too forward, but I was just complimenting you on your achievements thus far. No offense, OK?"

"None taken." She looked around me towards the fitness center. "Looks like you were working up quite a sweat yourself."

"Yeah. Something like that. Just trying to generate some new energy, that's all."

"You must be planning to use that energy at the stoplight party tonight, huh!" She laughed a bit and I joined her in amusement.

"You got jokes! I like that. But, to answer your question, yes, I'm planning to attend but I don't know about using any energy. And you? Will I have the pleasure of seeing you there?"

"I believe so. Dayna and I talked about it earlier so I think it's something we are keeping on our schedule."

"Well, then, I'll be sure to look for your color."

"Is that right?"

"Yes, it is. Is that OK with you?"

"We'll see." With that, she attempted to move past me. I playfully blocked her way and slowly eased to the side. She seized the opportunity and strolled down the long hallway.

I hurried to catch up to her. We both reached to press the 'up' button at the same time. I looked at her and laughed and she smiled at me.

Once we began to take our vertical ride, I asked her "So, what time do you plan to arrive?"

"Not really sure. What time should we be there?"

"I hope you arrive in time enough for me to enjoy your arrival." The ding signaled the arrival on one of the floors. One of the guests from level eight joined us. I would say them pressing that button was nothing more than blocking in my opinion. Since I no longer had space to flirt, I seized the moment to enjoy the bulging view behind her.

Just as I put the finishing touches on my edge up, there was a knock at the door. I knew it couldn't have been anyone other than Morgan because we agreed to meet up at ten so that we could go to the party together. Sure enough it was him.

He stepped in dressed like a walking traffic sign. As if the red t-shirt wasn't clear enough, he had somehow managed to find a pair of black pajama pants with red stop signs all over them, clearly indicating that he was completely off the market.

"Hurry up man. What's taking you so long?" I had retreated back to the bathroom area to detail my mustache and add some more wave cream to my hair.

"Shut your trap, man. It's only ten-fifteen which means you are just as late as I am."

"Anyways." He plopped down on the sofa and thumbed through one of the ESPN magazines that was on the coffee table.

"Let me take care of one more thing and I'll be ready." I splashed on a dab of Black Soul, smoothed my face and turned the light off. "I'm ready."

"Look at you man. You look like a reject joker from Batman!" He was talking about my green t-shirt and black pajama pants that I wore with some black and green plaid house slippers.

"Come on man and let's go!"

***

The party scene was already in full swing. For a moment there I thought I was in a real life game of red-light-green-light. The music was nice, the breeze was swift and the crowd was having a ball. After we ordered a few drinks – he a double shot of Johnny Walker Black and I a bottled water – we found a spot near the elaborate buffet and chilled. The bruhs were all over the place, too. I had a strong feeling that some of them were being very honest with the colors they were wearing. A few of them that I knew personally were jamming on the dance floor wearing green when in fact they should have been wearing all red from head to toe.

The event coordinators were rocking at the DJ booth. One of them got on the mic and summoned for all of the red lights to form two lines in preparation for a Caribbean version of the soul train line. You should have seen them. All the men were on one side and the ladies were on the other, sliding from left to right.

We moved closer to the action so that we could get a good look at the goings on. While there were a few yellows that made their way down the line, one of the event leaders challenged the green lights to a fierce twerking competition. A few of them had skills; some of them not so much.

Through the laughter and 'aww-yeahs' strolled the sexiest woman on the island – Vay. I slid closer to the line, pushing Morgan behind me. The way she lifted her hair high into the air and let it slide through her fingers as she dropped her hair back down. I watched her take a quick lesson from the dance leader and dirty-wind her hips down to the sand. She popped each of her protruding cheeks like a Magic City pro. No doubt the fellas were all over her, some within their limits and others that didn't have any business trying to push their limits. Everyone whooped and hollered. By the time she was finished everyone else was afraid to go behind her, but they managed to get through the line with at least a round of applause.

Her sister, Dayna, was having a little class of her own. She and a couple of other heavy duty beauties were two-stepping to the island version of *The Electric Slide*. Everyone was having the time of their lives.

The DJ put on a little something to slow things down a tad. Seeing my moment, I made my way to the gathering of women at the tiki bar. Morgan had managed to find another red to dance with. No doubt he was telling her some kind of joke because there was nothing funny about the lyrics to R. Kelly's *Slow Wind*.

"Good evening ladies." 'Good evening' they all said in unison. "Excuse me, ladies. Come with me, please." I grabbed Vay's hand and helped her down from the bar stool.

"Where are we going?"

"Vay –

"Please. My name is Nevaeh."

"Nevaeh?"

"Yes. Nevaeh."

"What a unique name. I like it."

"Thanks. It's 'heaven' spelled backwards."

No wonder. "You're very welcome. Well, Nevaeh, may I have this dance?"

"You may."

I led us to a more secluded area near the water line. We were still able to hear the music, but I wanted to be able to hear her voice more.

As we danced against one another, her head atop my chest, I couldn't help but notice a slight tremble. She barely said a word and neither did I. I was simply enjoying the moment and hoped she was doing the same.

"Vay. There is something I need to tell you."

She whispered, "what's that?"

After a slight moment of hesitation, I said, "From the first moment I noticed you, I couldn't help but wonder why you wore no ring on your finger. There is no way in the world no one had become the happiest and more fortunate man on the planet by not making you his wife. I mean, am I missing something?"

She lifted her head and looked at me. "If you're asking me am I married the answer is no."

"May I ask why not?"

"Because he hasn't found me yet. Besides, I'm not so sure that I am marriage material."

"What do you mean?" I continued to support her back and sway with her.

"I was in a relationship once and it didn't quite work out."

"So, you've given up on the idea of marriage because one male didn't appreciate the one-of-a-kind, priceless diamond that he had?"

"Not entirely, but I have thought about it."

"Come here - let's sit over here." I guided her to a large boulder that was flattened on the surface. "Watch your step." I removed my t-shirt and placed it on top for her to rest on. She felt around for the best place to sit and hopped on it. "Now, what do you mean, 'he hasn't found you yet?'"

"From what I can see and from my experiences, most men appear to be intimidated by me. For instance, I am the owner and CEO of my own consulting firm, I hold a bachelors, two masters degrees and numerous professional certifications. I own several properties including three cars, I have never been to jail, I don't have any addictions, and I have no children. But, the worst part about all of it is, the male pickings are extremely slim and my chances lessen the older I become." She lowered her head and bashfully turned away. "I'm sorry. I didn't mean for all of that to come out. You must think I'm some sort of desperate wanna-be housewife or something."

I laughed at her attempted joke. "No, no, no, that's OK. That's quite alright. I'm really enjoying listening to you." I decided to leave the marriage thing along – for now – and ask her, "Tell me more about your business. What exactly do you do?"

"I help companies and organizations look for the white space in their business operations."

"Continue, please."

"Well, I have to do a complete assessment of their policies and procedures, gain an understanding of their mission, vision and strategic plan – if they have one and if not help them develop one – in an effort to improve their overall bottom line in capital and personnel investments. I even conduct life coaching seminars to my clients' employees and serve as an adjunct professor at one of the local universities."

"No wonder he hasn't found you yet. You've got a lot going on, woman!"

She continued to provide more details about the difference between the services other consultants provided and what she does. And I listened. I listened as each word escaped between her plump, rose colored lips. I marveled at the way her hair blew in the wind. I reached for each strand as they snatched away from my grasp.

She looked in my direction and I reached for her face. Leaning closer to her, I rested my lips upon hers hoping and praying that my invitation would be accepted.

Immediately she withdrew. I waited for her to do an assessment of the situation as I knew she was doing when she began to rise on her toes and returned the initial favor. The ocean mist tickled our feet as we stood to enjoy our French connection. My hands slowly ran the course of her back down to her backside and waited. Her arms wrapped around my neck and deepened our exchange. I released her and we looked at each other.

We shared a smile. I couldn't stand looking at her any longer without looking at her with a look of explicit intent in my gaze. "Nevaeh, I know you don't know me and I don't know you, and I promise you I have *never* done anything like this before in my life, but I don't want this to end."

"I've never done anything like this either."

"My mother always told me that there is a first time for everything."

"And she would be right."

"Is this your first time in Aruba?"

"Yes."

"Mine, too." I grabbed her hands and kissed the inside of her palms.

"You're sure you're not married?" I asked.

"I think I would know if I were married or not, but to answer your question, no, I am not married."

"Nevaeh?

"Yes?"

"What do you say to enjoying a different kind of first? Together?"

She smiled and said, "Sure. Why not? You only live once, right?"

"YOLO!" With that, we turned and made our way through the crowd towards the hotel lobby. The partygoers were still raising the roof and having a good time and little did they know that we were on our way to have a good time of our own.

Chapter 16 - Nevaeh

'You only live once'. How bold of me to agree to have yet another first and with a man whom I hardly knew. For all I knew, his first name could have been Freddie and his last name could have been Kreuger. But, I didn't get that feeling. For the first time in a long time, I was beginning to feel again and in this feeling, I was willing to step outside of my comfort zone and do something wild and crazy for a change. I just hoped that what we were about to do wouldn't make me smile now and cry later.

We waded through the crowd of folks mixing and mingling. I had been so lost in my interlude with Chance that I hadn't seen which direction Dayna had gone. I tried to look for her as I approached the lobby, but I didn't see her anywhere.

We arrived at his fifteenth floor penthouse just moments after leaving the party. Upon entrance, I noticed how elaborately decorated the place was. This place was larger than most people's apartments.

He walked over to the media console and adjusted his iPod to Pandora and I made my way to a seat on the sofa.

The sounds of the neo-soul crooner Anthony Hamilton made his presence as I watched my soon-to-be opponent's every move, thinking about what was about to go down. He made his way from the living room to the kitchen then back to the living room.

"May I offer you something to drink?"

"I don't drink, but a bottled water would be nice."

"Me either." I smiled and she did the same. "That's the third thing we have in common, you know?"

"The third thing?"

"Yes. Neither of us drink, this is our first time in Aruba, and neither of us is married."

Hearing this made me smile if only for a moment. It wasn't until his comment that I noticed that he was wearing a green shirt. Needless to say, I would hope that he was being honest in his wardrobe selection. The only thing I remember were the arms of steel that snuggled against the sleeve of his shirt and the mountainous pecs of his bosom that stretched across the front of his massive body. The impression of his third leg was noticeably steeled against his thigh.

"Are you involved with anyone? Are you in a relationship?"

"No, Nevaeh. I'm not involved with anyone and I am not in a relationship...yet." I looked at him waiting for more.

"What does 'yet' mean?"

"It means, I have forever plans for you and me." With that last statement, he kissed me again, this time sliding his hand down the back of my shirt. I flinched at the touch of his ice cold hands.

He had grabbed a few glasses and a small bucket filled with ice and joined me on the sofa, sitting nearest the balcony door. "Is there anything else I can get for you?"

"No. The water is fine, thanks," I lied.

"So tell me, Nevaeh, are you sure you want to do this? I mean, I would completely understand if you didn't."

"I'm here, aren't I?"

"Indeed you are. But, I would be remised if I didn't tell you that I have wanted you since the moment I laid eyes on you. I knew that I had to meet you, and get to know you better. And just one more thing."

"What's that?"

"If I said that you have a sexy body – a body that I would love to make love to, a body that I would like to share with in a pleasurable moment between two consenting adults who are eager to lavish in the opportunity that lies between us, a body that I would absolutely love to hacer como mi comida libre durante la noche - would you hold it against me?"

"Wait, what was that? Say that again?" He smirked.

"It would be easier if I showed you."

He carefully placed the bottle of water I was holding on the table in front of me and grabbed my hands. He began to rise and I followed suit. The way he looked me in the eyes told me there was a passion that was rising in him that hadn't made an appearance in a long, long time.

I waited. He waited. He rested his chin on top of my head, wrapped his arms around me and we began to dance again. I stepped back from him and looked up into his eyes. The anchoring of my heavy heart had suddenly been lifted. Here I was standing with what seemed like a genuine member of the male species and all I could think about was the way he made me feel. I was extremely nervous, but I looked forward to the way I hoped he would make me feel in just a few moments.

"Nevaeh, I want you."

"Come get me then."

He spun me around and began to raise my emerald green fitted t-shirt over my head. I braced myself for the long overdue sensations and the rapid beating of my heart. I obliged his move with one of my own by extending his arms high in the air and removing his shirt. The chocolate mountains and valleys that greeted me increased the rhythm of my desire.

He kissed me softly and slowly as he palmed my pretty round brown. One breast and then the other found their way out of my bra and into his warm mouth. He suckled each nipple, first individually and then jointly. I hissed as my body temperature began to rise at the coolness of his tongue. As if he were reading my mind, he picked me up and straddled me around his waist and walked towards the bedroom. I thought he was going to just throw me down on the bed and go for what he knew, but instead he snatched the comforter off the bed with one hand while continuing to hold me with the other. We continued our kiss as we made our way to the balcony.

The artic breeze that tingled across my back was even more stimulating to other open areas of my region. I felt the comforter brush against my leg as it was dropped to the floor of the balcony. Gently, he laid me down on my back when all of a sudden it began to rain. One kiss after another consumed my lips, my cheeks on down to my neck. My peaks of pleasure beckoned for his touch.

Moments of his affection left me somewhat blinded. My touch sensations heightened as the brisk wind and blowing rain drops uninvitedly swept through the tiny space between us. The rivalry was real. After stretching one leg on top of the rail and the other on the bistro table, he lowered his head and inhaled the nectar of my sweetness. Not one for wanting to be outdone, he slurped me mightily and nibbled on my love button competing with the heavy downpour to see which could make me wetter. In and out, stronger and then deeper, he French kissed my private lips like it was nobody's business. He wallowed at the taste of my honey box, catching each drop from my budding center. I responded in the only way I knew how – moaning and groaning – until my poor body couldn't take it anymore. The sound of the crashing waves echoed as it sent a rambunctious spray of salt water in all directions just as I was doing the same. At the height of my excitement, he tried to control the jolting of my body and guarded my many attempts to escape from his grip as he now steadied my legs on his shoulders.

The poking of his manhood convinced me that I had prepared him just as much as my moistness revealed that he had prepared me. He parted each side of my womanly well, removed his weapon of mass seduction, and caressed my clit. Suddenly, I felt the warmth of his bulb arrive at my girly gate. I tried to steady my breathing, but the stimulation was too much to bear.

And that's when two became one.

I matched each of his strokes with a few of my own as he kept pounding. With each beat I became higher in ecstasy and I didn't want to come down. The intensity of our intimacy matured to a full-fledge art of engagement to dizzying capacities. His final thrust was sealed with an exchange of lust that closed the space between us.

Tears of satisfaction crept out of each eye as I tried to take in what just happened. I held his head against my shoulder as he reduced the speed of his breathing since crossing the finishing line.

Neither of us said a word. After a few moments, he was finally able to move. He stood before me, revealing the body of a champion who had just conquered the ultimate defeat. He helped me to my feet and guided my nakedness back into the living area. After closing the door, I followed him into the bedroom where I assumed round two was about to take place. Instead, he and I spooned diagonally across the bed and, unbeknownst to us both, drifted into the deepest slumber.

***

The rays of the sun poked and prodded at my eyelids. I tried to remember what happened the night before, but my memory escaped me. The stiffness of my body made me feel like I had been in a G.L.O.W. wrestling match, but the smell of something good cooking aroused my awakening.

"Good morning, beautiful!" Chance walked up to me and kissed me on the forehead. He sat on the side of the bed and smoothed my hair back out of my face. I had somehow been positioned under the covers, facing the second set of glass doors that led to the bedroom balcony.

"Good morning, Chance."

"How did you sleep? From the looks of things, I would say you slept pretty well," he said pointing to the small, gray streaks that decorated the side of my mouth.

"Oh, my goodness! I must look a mess!" I attempted to hide beneath the covers and he playfully snatched them back.

"That's OK, beautiful. I like the way you look no matter what."

With the soreness I felt, I slowly began to recollect the rendezvous that had taken place just a few hours earlier. "What time is it?"

"It's about eight thirty."

I turned around and looked at the alarm clock on the nightstand and sure enough it was almost nine o'clock. "Oh, no. I have to go. I know Dayna is worried sick about me."

"She's not. I called her earlier this morning and told her that you were with me and that you were safe."

"You did?"

"Yeah. Aside from me waking her up, she seemed quite pleased." He grinned and I marveled at his display of perfectly white teeth.

"I bet she did." I sat up slightly and leaned back on my arms. "What's that I smell that smells so good?"

"Well, I figured that you may have a hearty appetite after our meeting last night," he air quoted, "so, I ordered room service. I hope you don't mind some parmesan and herb stone ground grits, scrambled eggs, Cajun beef hash, turkey bacon, cream cheese biscuits, tropical fruit salad, and some freshly squeezed orange juice? There is also a small assortment of breakfast breads."

"Dang. All of that?"

"Yes. I wasn't sure about what you ate so I decided to order a variety of breakfast selections. But first, follow me, please. Your bath water is waiting for you."

"Bath water? How long have you been up?"

"A while." He grabbed me by the hand and led me to the Italian marble decorated vanity quarters.

I secured my hair with the hair claw that was lying next to the loofah sponge and stepped inside the sunken, round-shaped bathtub. Thoughts of the past twenty-four hours kept me company while I marinated in the milk and honey soak before cleansing my body from head to toe. I could hear some noises coming from the bedroom; it sounded like Chance was gift wrapping something.

I allowed my mind to take me to a place it had yet to visit in a long time. I thought about Chance's question regarding why I had never been married. The truth was I was afraid to be, but I believed I had every right to be.

So many people that I knew were simply getting married as if it were some sort of trend and wore the union of marriage as if it were some sort of accessory. Most of today's men and women thought of marriage as some sort of accessory you wore to a gathering of friends or to a New Year's Eve celebration or something. I was not one for wanting to become any man's wife just for the sake of saying 'I's married now'! And, I don't care what Beyoncé says because the ring doesn't mean a thing. That had never been appealing to me and I wasn't about to start now.

I was tired of giving my everything while always ending up with nothing. A man had to be fully committed unto the Lord and in the position to seek a virtuous woman and I wanted to be the only one whom he found. The way I saw it, the marital dynamics were often overlooked and that just wasn't acceptable to me. I wasn't in the business of being anyone's side chick and I dare not be any man's secret. Respect, honesty, faithfulness and communication had to be contributing factors for any relationship but they were key components for a successful marriage. And none of that would be possible without the good Lord above.

I broke out of my stupor and finished my bath. Afterwards, I stepped out of the jetted tub and put on the plushly, white robe that was hanging on the back of the bathroom door.

When I walked back into the room, I noticed an assortment of lotions, sprays and other hygienic toiletries spread across the dresser. A yellow, tube top maxi dress was sprawled across the bed complete with a matching panty and bra set. A pair of sandals was placed at the foot of the bed. By then, Chance had rejoined me.

"What in the world, Chance? All of this is for me?"

"What does it look like, Nevaeh? I couldn't have you walking around the hotel in your birthday suit now could I?" He grabbed the towel from my hand. "May I help you with this?" He untied the belt to the robe and slid it over my shoulders. I stepped away from the robe when he took a seat on the edge of the bed.

"How did you know my size?"

"With a sexy body like yours, I just let my hands do the measuring for me last night during our late night encounter. Come closer so that I can check to make sure that I was accurate in my measurements."

He began to pat my skin with the towel, absorbing any remaining water drops. As I stood before him, I couldn't help but continue to think about the way he made me feel and how much I would like to feel that way again with him. Seeing my expression just as he neared my triangle of love, he separated my legs to allow more room for the towel to go between them. He paused.

I placed my hands on his shoulder and pushed him back on the bed. I straddled his jean-covered manhood and began to kiss him passionately. He cupped my naked body and swiftly lifted me forward into a seated position over his face. As I enjoyed his personal definition of face time, I held my head and moved with the motion of sheer excitement. He caressed my chocolate domes from beneath me giving full attention to my Hershey's kisses. Just as my moment of pleasure began to intensify, he flipped me forward, positioning me on my stomach.

I immediately heard the sounds of his belt buckle becoming undone followed by the chattering of the teeth of his zipper. I rose backwards to the occasion as he assumed his position. He connected with me instantly. The pounding of his body against mine sent multiple pains of pleasure to the center of my core. When I sensed a slight moment of hesitation I crawled away from him and threw him down on the bed. I thrilled in the glow of his surprise at my maneuver to show him a few tricks of my own. I didn't waste any time mounting him and I rode him into the sunset of our journey. At our conclusion, he laid in the

L.C. AMOS

crook of my arm as I graced his head a few times with the palm of my hand.

After a quick shower, we got dressed and joined one another at the bistro table on the balcony to consume the breakfast that he ordered. One could only wonder what was going through his head about me. I definitely didn't want to come off as if this is something I did on the regular, because it wasn't, but just when I was about to break the silence, he beat me to the punch.

"Thank you for allowing me to make your acquaintance, Nevaeh."

"Likewise." We raised our juice glasses and toasted to a mutually agreed upon understanding.

"I would like to share something with you if I may." I nodded and gave him my attention. "I really hope we didn't move too fast. As I shared with you earlier, this is the first time I have ever done something like this. One of the reasons I am telling you this is because one, I don't want you to think this is something I do on the regular and two, I want you to know that in no way, shape or form do I think any less of you as a woman for the same thing. The way I see it, we are a man and a woman, two consenting adults, that saw something that we both wanted and we supported each other's interest. Does that sound about right?"

I finished a sip of juice and answered, "Yes, it does. I would say you summed it up perfectly."

"Not quite."

"Oh, how so?"

"Well, you see," he took a sip of water and leaned forward against the table, "I really don't want this to end. I

148

want to see you again and again and again. That's if you will let me."

"How can you be so sure?"

"How could I not?"

Oo-wee. "Well, we've only known each other for what, a few days?"

"And, I would like to take a few more days, weeks, and months to get to know you better." He reached across the table and grabbed my hand. "Nevaeh, listen to me. In my profession I am faced with making critical yet intelligent decisions every day. In my field, there is no room for error. So, I have to be strategic in my professional brilliance in order to yield the most positive results of that decision."

"I see. Your profession sounds quite interesting. So, what exactly is it that you do?"

Just then the phone rang and interrupted our conversation. "Excuse me, let me see who this is. It's probably Morgan."

I finished my fruit while he finished the call. By the time he had returned, I was standing to knock any loose crumbs from my dress. "Look, I have really enjoyed my time spent with you, but I must leave you now."

"I understand. So, have you thought about what I said?"

"I have. Thank you for the clothes and the breakfast and the – "

"Don't forget the midnight snack!" he interrupted. I blushed at his reminder.

"And the midnight snack."

"By the way, I had your pajama romper dry cleaned. It was returned this morning before you woke up. It's hanging in the coat closet by the door."

I smiled at his meticulousness. "Thanks again, Chance!"

"Absolutely. It's been my pleasure, Nevaeh." I walked towards the entrance to remove my dry cleaning from the closet with Chance close on my heels.

"Until next time." I flicked my hair across my shoulders one last time to make sure I was presentable upon my exit.

"So, there will be a next time, huh?" He leaned against the closet door.

"Yes. There will be a next time!"

"What do you say that you accompany me to the formal finale tomorrow tonight?"

"Sure. I guess that will be OK."

"I'll come get you around say seven-thirty. Maybe Morgan can keep Dayna company and we can all have a good time."

"That sounds good. I'm sure she wouldn't mind. I'll see you then." We kissed and I headed back to my room.

Chapter 17 - Dayna

I was still in the bed when Vay came back. I knew it couldn't have been anyone but her because I placed the 'do not disturb' sign on the door last night mainly for the hotel staff.

"Dayna? Where you at girl?" Vay walked into the bedroom where I was lying on my back. She could tell that I had been crying. "Dayna! Oh, my gosh. What's wrong with you?"

I mustered enough energy to respond. "Not soon after we got to the party last night, I felt extremely nauseous, my head started hurting real bad and the chest pains were unbearable."

"Chest pains!" she screamed.

"Yes, chest pains. I tried to overlook them for as long as I could, but I didn't want to ruin the night for you, Vay. You were so excited about going to the party last night so I forced my way through the discomfort."

"No, Dayna! You should have said something. I must admit that I didn't notice anything wrong because if I had we would have stayed here or taken you to see a doctor or something."

"I know. That's why I stayed long enough to see you do your thing in the Caribbean soul train line. Once I saw you talking to ol' boy that we met the other night, I knew that you were going to be OK and I came back to the room to lie down for a bit to see if the pain would subside. I had planned on going back out, but that didn't happen."

"I don't know about this, Dee. Something is not right. Are you telling me everything?"

I looked at her with the side eye and rose slightly. "Yes, I'm telling you everything!" I lied. The nauseating feeling returned just as I began to sit up straight and I eased my way back down. What I wasn't telling her was that I began to feel these pains long before now. They came from out of nowhere. It was earlier this morning when they began to get increasingly stronger with each waking minute. I had to fake it even harder when Chance called to tell me that Vay had stayed with him last night and that she was OK. I knew that if I let on that I wasn't feeling well that he would have indeed told Vay and she would have come running to rescue just as she always does. I wanted her to have some fun for a change and do something for herself.

"Maybe we should call you a doctor or something. I'm worried about you."

"Look. I'll make you a deal. If I don't feel any better within the next few hours then we'll do just that. Deal?"

"Deal."

Less than two hours after I had made a deal with Vay, the pain began to worsen again. Seeing this, she sprang into action and decided to call the front desk to summon a medic to our room. From her report, she was told that the medical doctor would not return to the island until Monday. Being that it was Saturday, Monday would be too late, I thought. They did, however, send a nurse on staff to our room. After I was administered a vinegar and Alka-Seltzer concoction to help with the chest pains and nausea, the nurse provided me with syrup that would help me to rest.

Early the next morning, Vay informed me that she had called the airline last night to have our departure flight changed from Monday to Sunday en route back to Charlotte. She had all of our bags packed and had made arrangements for a taxi service to take us to the airport. As luck would have it, Meego was our departing driver as well.

Just as we were loading into the taxi, I noticed Chance and some other gentleman jogging in place just in front of the main entrance. Vay had gone back inside to formally check us out of the room when they approached the sliding doors.

"Nevaeh! What's going on? Are you leaving? I know you're not leaving?" Chance asked. His partner waited in tow and looked on.

"Hey. Yes, we need to leave. We're headed back home. It was nice meeting you."

He tried to call out to her to stop and tell him what was going on, but by then she had joined me in the cab and we were pulling off heading towards the airport.

***

We caught one of Rev. Marks' online sermons while in flight. We prayed mightily for my healing and strength and were both still high in the spirit when we landed at Charlotte-Douglas International Airport just after nine o'clock. I immediately asked Vay to take me home. The only thing I wanted to do was to lie down and rest, even though the pain wasn't getting any better. After she saw that I wasn't going let up, she obliged and did just as I had asked.

As soon as we pulled into the driveway, I noticed Braylon's car wasn't home. This was probably a good thing because one, it meant that he wouldn't be overly worried about me and two, I could get some rest in my own bed.

"Let me call Braylon and Synatra to let them know that we are back."

"I'll call them, Dayna. I'll call Jessica and everybody else, too. All I need you to do is to get some rest until the doctor is able to see you. I'm going to try to get you an appointment first thing in the morning." She placed my luggage in the foyer and helped me upstairs to my room.

"Hey. I'm going to need to borrow your car; I need to run by the house and the post office to check our mailboxes," she said.

"Vay?"

"I will be sure to come and get you in the morning for your appointment with Dr. LeGare and I'll have Syn take me back to my car. Is that cool?"

"Sure, girl. What a silly question."

She carefully tucked me in and kissed me on the forehead. It wasn't too much longer after she left that I drifted off as well. The peace and quiet of the house helped to relax me even further than the pain medicine I took so I was sure to take full advantage.

Chapter 18 - Adrian

I was glad I decided to take off a little bit early today. I wanted to make sure that I laid the foundation for my night out with Synatra. I had to be honest with myself. I couldn't stop thinking about the night we shared a few weeks back. I thought about her the rest of the night.

I had promised myself that I wouldn't get involved with anyone anytime soon, but that had been three years ago. To me, it seemed better to be emotionally unavailable rather than risk getting my heart handed to me again. But, there was something about her and I had a good feeling about what I was about to do.

Though her wanna-be hard exterior is one of the things that captured my attention in the first place I could see right through her. That type of girl always caught my attention back in the day, but with time and maturity, that desire had lessened tremendously. She wasn't nearly as daring as she pretended to be. I could see that she had a hurting heart, the kind that never knew the protection of her father or the kind that had never felt the love from a mother. I was beginning to feel like if I didn't let her know sooner than later that I would miss out on my chance to make her my woman.

I adjusted my iPod to an old school 90's R&B station while I took my shower. I had planned on taking her to this nice restaurant on the lake but decided against it. Instead, I had hired an executive chef to prepare an exclusive dinner for us aboard the Lake Norman Dynasty. After dinner, our evening would conclude by spending an evening under the stars amid the lakes.

I dialed Synatra's number and placed the call on speakerphone waiting for her to answer. It always did my heart good when I heard her voice.

"Hey, Adrian. What's good with you?"

"Hey, sweetness. How are you?"

"I'm good. I'm good. So, what's up? Where we going?"

"Be easy, love. Take your time."

"Love? Where all that come from?"

"We'll talk about that later. You about ready?"

"Yeah. Umm, let me just put the finishing touches to my hair and I'm all set."

"Cool. I'm about finished as well. I'll be by your place to pick you up, say, in another fifteen minutes. Give me your address."

"Ummmm, why don't you come pick me up from the restaurant?"

"That's a little unofficial isn't it? Why can't I come pick you up from your house?"

"'Cause."

"'Cause what? If you are worried about whether or not I'm going to stalk you or something I'm not." She hesitated. I could almost hear her thinking. "Look, I just want the night to go as planned, if that is OK with you?"

"Yeah, well. I'ma put it to you like this. If I catch you following me home, uninvited, or hiding out in my bushes, I'ma have that ass dealt wit', ya heard me?"

Although she couldn't see me, I shook my head at her bullying. "I hear you, Synatra. The address?"

"I live in south Charlotte, off I-85. I'm at 3465 Twirling Ridge Park."

"Great. I'll see you in a minute." I put the finishing touches on my look, checked for any last minute particulars I needed to tend to and headed out the door.

Once on the highway, I thought about what I might actually be getting myself into. The one thing I did know is that I was into her and I was sure she was into me. I wanted to make this evening special for her and that's exactly what I planned to do.

The Twirling Ridge community looked like something out of a parade of houses magazine. On either side of the road were large, brick framed homes that possessed no less than four car garages. The immaculate landscaping suggested that year round treatments were a priority and greatly improved the curb appeal. I drove slowly through the development until I approached 3465. I pulled into the driveway and took one last breath before killing the ignition.

Nothing but silence surrounded me as I shut the door. I took a quick look around, admiring the posh surroundings. Just as I reached to push the doorbell, the door swung open. Standing before me was a queen filled with extraordinary beauty. I scanned her physique from head to toe. I stared at the way she struck her pose in the doorway. I almost forgot why I was there.

"You look amazing!"

"Thank-ya, thank-ya! You 'ont look so bad yourself, playa."

"Thank you."

"You ready?"

"Yes. Don't forget to lock everything up."

"Oh, I got this."

She closed the door and followed behind me. I grabbed her hand to assist her down the steps watching her step with a walk of grace. Once she was in the car securely, I kissed the back of her hand and shut the door. Before I backed out, she aimed her phone at the house after pressing a few buttons.

Just as sure as I had thought, her curiosity got the best of her she asked me, "So, is this your ride? I've never seen you in this at the job." Synatra was referring to my onyx black E-Class.

"Yes. This is my car."

"Nice."

She didn't say anything more about the car, but I could only imagine what was going through her head. I wasn't going to offer any more information if she didn't ask, at least not at the moment.

"So, where are you taking me?"

"It's a surprise."

"A surprise? But, what if I don't do surprises?"

"Trust me. You'll enjoy this surprise." I entered the highway heading further south en route to Lake Norman. "Now, hush, woman and enjoy the ride."

Thirty minutes later we were pulling into the Dynasty docking zone. I parked in one of the spaces and made my way around the car to let her out. I was careful to watch her expression as she looked in awe at the gigantic yacht.

"Damn. That's fly right there."

"Come with me, please."

"Wait. We going on there? Word! I can dig it."

As we embarked, the maître de met us midway up the ramp. "Misseur Cooper, Madame Jones, this way please."

Everything was exactly as we planned. The dining room was decked out in celebrity fashion. The soft lighting bounced off the golden chandelier above us. The centerpiece raised the impression of the ambience. Noticing a table set for two, I could tell that she was thoroughly fascinated with the set up.

The maître de summoned her to be seated and extended her chair. She gracefully took her seat and placed her purse in his waiting hand.

After we received our welcome from the executive chef, he reviewed the menu he was preparing.

"Again, I am Chef Javian King and I am more than happy to make your acquaintance this evening. May I start you off with a beverage?"

"Synatra, what would you like?"

"Will you order for us, please?" A sudden expression of uncertainty painted her face. It was a look I had never seen on her before.

"Certainly, Chef. We'll have a bottle of your finest champagne."

"Celebrating a special occasion I see. I have just the thing."

We could barely feel any movement as we disengaged from the dock. No sooner had we began to make strides in the lake, the Chef returned with a bottle of New England '25. He filled our flutes and placed the bottle in the ice bucket.

"Synatra, you look a little troubled. Is everything OK?"

"Yeah, I mean, yes. Everything is fine." She noticed me notice her self-correction. I didn't say anything about it, keeping my thoughts to myself.

"I'm glad." We made small talk and everything was going just fine until she asked me the one question I had dreaded since the day she hired me.

"Can I ask you something, Adrian?"

"You may."

"What you get locked up for?"

"Why do you ask?"

"I just want to know. And just so you will know, your answer will have no bearings on your employment. Truthfully, I saw that you checked 'yes' on your application and that was enough for me at the time. I figured if you were honest enough to tell me that you had been convicted I really wasn't gonna push the issue. I mean, I don't know anyone that would have checked 'yes' if the answer was really 'no'."

"Let's just enjoy the evening, shall we?

"Nah, man. Come on, Adrian. I want to know. I really want to know."

"I knew this day would come. You sure about that?"

"I wouldn't have asked you if I didn't. The truth, please."

For many years I had suppressed that memory until now. In the moments before I revealed to her for the first time ever my reason for being locked up, I hesitated. I hesitated because I didn't know what would be found on the other side of my truth. I wasn't quite sure if she would keep her word and not use my revelation against me or if she would begin to treat me differently because of what happened. A part of me was glad she finally asked me because I knew it was only a matter of time.

And thus, I began to answer her.

"I grew up in a poverty stricken, rough side of Detroit. The kind of living that kept you on the floor praying and hoping bullets weren't going to come flying through the windows. It was definitely no place to raise a family. My father knew that all too well.

"That Sunday afternoon when my father abandoned us, my mom was preparing dinner when she noticed that she was short on eggs for the cake she was baking. He told her he would go to the store to get a dozen and he never came back. She really believed that he would return, even after she waited for more than seven hours. Days went by, weeks flew by and nothing.

"My mom slipped into a deep depression after that. You see she had moved from Philly to Detroit to be with him because he said that he would take care of her. She was tired of Philly anyway so she thought it was a good opportunity for the both of them. He was a truck driver that earned a pretty good penny so the notion didn't seem all that unusual to her.

"About five years after that, my mom went out with some friends and met a guy named Ronald at one of the local pool halls. Everybody in the hood knew him as "Doo-Ronnie". Doo-Ronnie was the type of guy that was known to be a liar, a cheat and a thief and sometimes he was all of those things at the same time. It didn't take long for game to recognize game. I knew he was bad news from the moment he stepped foot in our house.

"The first time he hit her, she bled for a whole week out of her left ear. She refused to go to the hospital because she didn't want him to get in trouble. Time after time my brother and I had tried to convince her to leave him. He was no good for her. He was no good for any of us. But, she insisted on him staying. She used to say things like 'but I love him' and 'he said we're going to get married one day'. The truth of the matter is I think she didn't leave him because she didn't want to be alone.

"That night in the summer of '92 marked the end of life as I knew it. My mom had just gotten home from work and was preparing dinner. I had been dealing with a headache all day at work so the first thing I wanted to do was to get away from all of the noise. The severity of my migraine had gotten the best of me so I took a pill and went to lie down in hopes of the pain subsiding. I was hurting so badly I passed out across the bed. I didn't even remember falling asleep.

"Not even an hour later, a loud bang had awakened me. I recognized the voice of my mother's boyfriend. He was yelling at her, calling her all kinds of names. She was yelling back at him, too, demanding that he keep his voice down so as to not wake me up. But, it was too late. I got up and was making my way down the steps when I saw him deliver a mighty blow to her face. He punched her so hard she flew across the living room and fell back and hit the side of her head on the corner of an old floor model radio credenza. And I snapped. The next thing I knew, I was on top of him delivering blow after blow after blow until I eventually, and unbeknownst to me at the time, beat him to death with my bare hands. The next door neighbor, Choco, ran over and tried his best to pull me off of him, but his strength was no match for my fury. He later texted my younger brother to let him know what was going on. I, on the other hand, was headed to jail.

"See, Choco knew all too well about Doo-Ronnie. Doo-Ronnie had dated his mom some years back and had treated her the same way. After he put her in the hospital for nearly beating her to death, she finally decided to wise up and she left him. Choco once told me that the only reason why he thought that Doo-Ronnie had taken an interest in my mom is because he found out that we moved right next door to one of his old girlfriends. I guess it was his way of trying to make Miss Volandra jealous or something.

"After I was able to calm down and kind of think things through, it came to me and I remembered what sparked the argument. He tripped out on her because she didn't give him the biggest piece of chicken; she was saving it for me.

"At the time of the incident, he was in violation of a 50-B protection order anyway that my mom had imposed on him which was active for a minimum of ten years. They were just into month two of the order when everything happened.

"My mom died on the way to the hospital in the back of the ambulance. Seeing that I had no prior convictions, and I had never been to jail, the judge sentenced me to eight years for involuntary manslaughter. I only served four. The only reason why I didn't receive a sentence longer than that was because I didn't use a weapon, but there was also no record of domestic violence on file for him.

"And so, I did my time. By myself. I used the time to think and I did lots of it. I thought about a lot of 'what ifs' and I sang the 'shoulda, coulda, woulda' song. I wished for this and I hoped for that. But, through it all, if I had it to do all over again, I would do the same thing.

"My mother worked hard to put food on our table and clothes on me and my brothers back and to make sure we had a roof over our head. She instilled values and planted seeds of integrity and morality in us. That's something that I have never departed from, except for that one time. I hated seeing my mother with him. I knew he was no good for her. But, I guess after my father left she settled for the next thing that came her way. There had been others, others that weren't so mean and abusive, but for some reason she was stuck on him.

"I received a letter from Choco's mom, telling me that my brother came by the house the next day wanting to get showered and changed. He couldn't stand the fact of being in the house where his mom was abused. He borrowed some money from her and she hasn't seen him since. The cousin of one of my former cell mates told me they had seen him in Durham, North Carolina but, that's been years ago and I haven't heard from him or seen him since he left that morning."

Soft music reminded me that I was actually on a date with Synatra. Her silence led me to believe that she was having second thoughts about being on the boat with me. I waited for her to respond and I got nothing. Leaning back, I aimed my fingers upwards in a pistol position and rested my chin in the crook of my hands.

While she examined what I had just told her, I studied her facial expression, looking for any sign that indicated she was about to go off the deep end.

Instead, she said, "Damn, Adrian. That's so sad. I am so sorry you had to go through that." She shook her head slightly. As I reached for my glass to get a sip of water, she gripped my hand and squeezed it lightly and matched her act of sentiment with an empathetic smile.

Chef King waited for us to complete our moment of intimacy before approaching our table with a couple of mixed greens house salads.

Through moments of bad memories and a storied past, we moved from my personal revelation and engaged in some real grown folk conversation. I learned more about her and she learned more about me, as if the reason behind my previous incarceration weren't enough. It was extremely pleasing to spend an evening with her free from team meetings, inventory reports and business operations. We laughed, slapped each other high fives and flirted with each other all night long.

Just as we completed our meal and the sun was primed to turn in for the night, I stood and walked over to the railing near the bow of the vessel and she joined me. I held her in front of me and inhaled her scent that was sensually placed in the crook of her neck. She eyed the stars in the sky and let out a soft sigh.

"What's wrong? Are you cold?"

"A little."

"Here. Let me get closer to you." I eased her further into my body and hugged her waist a little tighter. "Is this better?"

"Much better."

I began to notice a sudden softness appear in her demeanor. That petite sized lady of rage had suddenly become a body of calmness. This transition sparked yet another level of interest in me.

"What's on your mind, baby?"

"Nothing." *Baby?*

"Uh oh."

"What?"

"Usually when a woman says 'nothing' it is usually 'something'. So, I ask you again, what's on your mind, baby?"

She faltered for a moment; I would imagine contemplating whether to put her cards on the table or to simply tell me what she thought I wanted to hear. "This has been an amazing night, Adrian. Thank you."

"You're very welcome."

"This night feels special, like I'm in a fairytale that never ends."

"It doesn't have to if you don't want it to."

"What you mean?"

"You'll see."

"Another surprise?" She leaned away from me to get a good look at my face.

"I guess you could say that."

"You are just full of 'em, huh? What have I done to deserve all of this?"

I purposely allowed the space between her question and my answer to grow.

"Synatra, there is something else I need to tell you. If you will spare me a few more moments of your time, I need to come clean with you about something."

"I'm listening." *Aw, hell. Here we go.*

The ripples in the water continued to span on either side of the cruiser. For the next few minutes, I exposed my hand and told her about how much I truly cared for her. She found out that shortly after I began working at the restaurant, I had fell completely in love with her. I never bothered to approach her because I didn't want to mix business with pleasure. I had never done anything like this before and I wasn't sure if she was willing to entertain a workplace relationship with an ex-convict like me. Confident I am, but I had to be more realistic than anything because the odds were definitely not in my favor from society's perspective. I had to feel her out. See what she was about.

Day after day, I watched her, learned more about her, and internalized her presence. Each day she became my favorite moment.

As it turns out, she had a few surprises of her own. She had been feeling the same way about me all along. And like me, she held back on making any sudden moves so as to not ruin our professional relationship. I wonder if that's why she always gave me an exceptional ranking during my performance evaluation and promoted me through the ranks so fast.

"Well, I'm glad to see we have a little more in common." She leaned forward and kissed me on the tip of my nose.

Just then, the knots were downshifted and we moved at a snail's pace. The release of the anchor made her flinch. The maître de returned to escort us to the debarkation location.

The lantern lit sidewalk curved towards the entrance of a beautiful, glass wrapped lakefront property.

"Adrian, what -? What is all of this? Whose house is this?"

"It's mine."

"Yours?" *How the hell can he afford all of this?*

"Yes, mine, woman!"

"But, I thought you lived over on Hemmingway?"

"And you would be right. But, I also have this property as well."

"Is there anything else you need to tell me tonight 'cause this is all just a bit too much, too fast, and too soon!" She snickered a little.

"Follow me. And just so you will know, there are more surprises, and our evening has officially begun." I playfully pecked her on the lips and held her hand steady as we walked up the pavement.

Chapter 19 - Synatra

For as long as I have lived in Charlotte, I have never been on, let alone dined, on the Lake Norman Dynasty and tonight he made that happen for me. It's not like I didn't have the money to do it, but I simply didn't have a companion with whom to do it. And, I was just too fly to be on some dinner yacht by myself.

I had to give ol' boy his props, though. Here I was thinking I was doing him and society a favor by hiring him and reducing the recidivism rate, when in fact he was teaching me a thing or two about being judgmental and believing in second chances. I dare not ask him where all of this money was coming from, although I had been thinking it ever since he picked me up. It never crossed my mind that he was stealing from the restaurant or anything. He was too honest for that, if there ever was such a thing. But, seeing this beautiful, gorgeous lake house was impressive.

He led me up the sidewalk and we entered the house. The foyer was warm and inviting with the way the wild floral arrangements spewed from the gold wall sconces that highlighted each wall at the entrance. The living room showed signs of an MTV crib inspired theme with its cream colored suede sectional that curved in front of the roaring fire place. The smoke grey statues and flaming red and mirrored home accent pieces added just the right amount of spunk to the atmosphere. Flames of heat stretched for the common area through the crackling of the fireplace. As if that wasn't enough, the baby grand piano that was posted in front of the floor to ceiling window that led to a patio sparkled like a twice-polished shellac set of acrylic nails.

I checked my phone for the time.

"Do you have somewhere else to be? Are you expecting a call?"

"No. Neither."

"Oh. Just wondering, 'cause you won't be needing that tonight, unless you plan to call the cops on me."

"Listen at you, taking control of the situation." I smiled. "Nice!" I silenced my phone and put it back in my purse.

"Do you want anything to drink? Some Moscato, perhaps?"

I had gotten lost in the experience. "I do."

"Ummh...you need to be careful how you say that!"

"Say what?"

"'I do.'"

"Is that right?"

"Yes. It is." He paused. "I've got a chilled, fresh fruit tray if you would like something to nibble on."

"Now who needs to careful about the way they say something." He cut his eye at me and handed me a glass of wine.

"Come on. Let me show you around the house."

My heels struck the hardwood floors as we strolled down the hallway. Room after room gave a glimpse into the life of a man by whom I had only known as Adrian Cooper. It was true what they said – never judge a book by its cover – but I had judged him by the pages of his life as well, which up until this point had been blank to me. The things he shared with me at dinner, the stories he told me about his life presented a different picture of him. It was a picture that I could stare at all day. No longer was he the guy who worked for me. Nope. He was slowly but for surely becoming the guy who worked for me that swept me off my feet.

Returning to the living room, he grabbed a tiny, flat remote and aimed it at the wall. Just then a partition separated and out folded a set of speakers. Simultaneously, the smooth jazz sounds of Jill Scott's *"So in Love"* began to fill the room. He began to groove a little bit and invited me to join him for a little two-step challenge. I did my thing and he tried to out-do me with his thing, but there was no competition. We took turns lip synching to one another, acting like we were a true duet.

Suddenly, he grabbed me and pulled me close to him and I was thankful that he did because I had wanted to do the very same thing all night long. His recess gave me a moment to collect myself. I graced the back of his head and returned the gaze.

He slowly began to undue the zipper from the back of my LBD. His soft kisses to my neck and shoulders gave me a flirtatious wave of chills. Without another second's notice, his hands were all over me. Up and down and up and down his hands combed my body in search of all of my sweet spots.

With no less than an act of accuracy, he removed his shoes and his shirt quickly and was approaching me again for his next act of play. My body began to want him more and more and he found out just how much when he lifted me onto his hips. I began to kiss him deeply, producing untapped desires he never knew he had. We played for a bit before he decided to take things to another level. By the time he returned from the kitchen, I was already lying naked on my side against the mink-like rug in front of the fireplace, ready and waiting.

"Put this on for me, please."

"This is different." I grabbed the scarf from him and folded it a couple a times. "Now, you ain't gonna handcuff me or nothing and torture me are you?"

"That remains to be seen, or in your case, unseen. Put it on, please." I complied.

He laid me on my back and after instructing me to place my arms by my side and straighten my legs, he waited. He waited for me to totally relax my mind, body and soul. It was kind of hard to do because I was ready for him to make me confess some of my wrongdoings from the tenth grade. Instead he waited and watched the heartbeat in my chest rise and fall, my breathing pacing with anticipation.

Then, he touched me.

I flinched at the caress of the finger that traced my forehead and down the bridge of my nose. He continued on that middle path until he found my sweet spot. There, he lightly tapped on the knob at the entrance of my lover's den. My body shivered and shook, but I naughtily wanted more. Just then, I felt the cold, wet texture of a piece of fruit on my lips that I quickly identified as a strawberry. That piece was followed by a pineapple ring and then a juicy slice of a peach. The taste testing game got a little interesting when I felt his digits invade my cum pocket. That same finger made its way to my lips. I refused to back down from a challenge with this dude, so I accepted it and slurped every ounce of me from it. This must have turned him on because the next thing I knew, he was straddling me and rubbing on my bangers. He licked my lips and lapped up the remainder of my essence.

The repeated injections of his erection instigated the freak in me. I bent my legs towards him, allowing him to go deeper. The removal of his rod provided me a brief space to collect my breathing, but that didn't last long. I wanted him. I wanted him badly, and that's exactly what he gave me. I allowed his shoulders to support my lower limbs as his head found its way to the center of my being. He spelled all four verses of the star spangled banner in English and Spanish with his tongue until my bomb burst in the air. I tried to escape but, I couldn't and the truth is I really didn't want to.

The warmth of my walls quickly began to melt the ice cube he planted inside me. He followed close behind. Cool droplets of condensation teased my thumper with every measured stroke. He cupped my rump to achieve a greater pump of passion and desire and all I could do was hold on for dear life.

After a cooling down period, we exchanged a look of love and continued to glow in gratitude. While he went to start the shower, I thought about what had just happened. For the second time, I was completely enamored with his bedroom skills. He certainly knew how to please a woman. I wasn't sure if that was because he was well practiced or he just had a knack for pleasuring women. This drew me closer to him for sure. Hell, I even broke my cardinal rule for him: never sleep with a man on the first date. Except for me, this rule was broken twice. Shame on me. But, he surprised me. He had great conversational skills, a very fun and outlandish personality. He seemed to be an extremely sweet guy and I was feeling him. He always paid mad attention to me and was very respectful of my feelings. My heart beat to a different tune whenever I was with him, let alone be around him. Before we started hanging out, I hadn't really paid that much attention to him in a I-wanna-be-your-woman type of way. Now, I can't get enough of him.

But, there was one thing about him that I couldn't quite put my finger on. He had this wall up that surrounded him. We all have secrets, but it wasn't his darkest side that scared me. It was the fact that he kept it hidden that did.

Then out of nowhere he said, interrupting my thoughts, "Synatra, I'm falling in love with you."

I didn't know how to respond to that. Sure, we had flirted heavily and talked often but up until this point, I never thought that he would feel the way he felt towards me so soon. It didn't matter if he told me that he had been thinking about me 'cause I just found that shit out tonight! We talked about one another and the fact that this level of mutual affection was the start of something new for us both. I was secretly enjoying the attraction that we shared, perhaps a bit more than I let on. But I couldn't help it. Adrian as of this date, this moment, became my man and I became his woman.

Chapter 20 - Nevaeh

I punched in the number to Dr. Legare's office and waited for one of the nurses to answer so that I could make Dayna's appointment. The good news is they were able to see her at two this afternoon. The double beeps let me know that my phone was about to die. It wasn't until then that I realized that I had left my charger at the hotel.

Afterwards, I placed a call to mom to one, let her know that we were back and two, to let her know about Dayna.

"Hey, baby. Where are y'all at? Where is Dayna?"

"We just got home, mom." I could tell by the urgency in her voice that something was wrong. "What's wrong, mom?"

"Are you driving?"

"Yes."

"Have you seen the news?"

"No." What is it? Tell me what's wrong."

After a slight pause, she breathed out a heavy sigh and said, "Honey, it's Braylon."

"What about Braylon? What's going on?

"He's in the hospital and it's not looking too good.

"Wait, what? What do you mean he's in the hospital and it's not looking too good?"

"I think you and Dayna need to get here as fast as you can."

"Well, that's what I was calling to tell you." I checked my mirror on the right before I merged over. "Where are you?"

"Your daddy and I are already here at Carolinas Medical. What did you have to tell me?"

"Dayna. It's Dayna, mom."

"Oh, Lord. What's wrong with her?"

"We had to cut our trip short because she suddenly became ill. I'm not sure if it's the Norovirus or something but she needs to go see a doctor. I've already made her an appointment for this afternoon, but it looks like I will have to cancel it." I let my free hand fumble through the armrest looking for Dayna's car charger but was unsuccessful. "What happened to Braylon?"

"Where is she now?"

"She's at home and you're not answering me. What happened to Braylon, Mom?"

"I'll fill you in when you get here. In the meantime, I'm going to need you to drive carefully, go get Dayna and the two of you get here as soon as you can."

"But, what –"

"There is no time for questions right now, Vay. Just do what I told you to do. Go and get Dayna and I'll see you when you get here. I love you and be careful."

All kinds of thoughts were running through my mind. Had anyone else tried to contact her? Had she found out what had happened? What was really going on with her?

I attempted to dial out to call her to let her know that I was on my way back to her house to get her, but the phone buzzed and quickly went dead. Having no communication at a time as critical as this had me wondering how any of us ever got along without mobile phones in the first place.

Twenty minutes later I pulled into the driveway, leaving the engine running. I bammed on the door for several minutes, but there was no answer. I went back to the jeep and laid on the horn, hoping that would get her attention. Just as I went to wail on it one more time, the front door opened.

Dayna apparently had been sleep. I could tell by the way she shielded her eyes from the sun rays and leaned lazily on the door frame. "Where is the fire?"

"Get your things. We need to leave."

"Leave? For what? Girl, my chest is still hurting."

"Dayna Yvonne Jones-Walters, I need for you to get yourself together now! We need to leave!" I yelled. Hearing me call her by her full name, she knew I meant business.

"What's wrong? Did something happen to Mom? Dad? Oh, my gosh! Is there really a fire? What is it?" The panic she displayed jumped off of her and onto me because her reaction reminded me that the answer I had – which was 'I don't know – would have been of no more comfort to her than not answering any of her questions at all. My only mission was to get her in the jeep and head towards the hospital to find out what had happened to her husband, my brother-in-law, Braylon.

"Please, just get in."

She looked at me strangely and finally said, "Let me turn off the TV and set the alarm. I'll be right there."

A few moments later she was making her way down the steps, using the hand rail for support. I opened the passenger side door and waited for her to hop in. I immediately ran around to the other side and hurriedly clicked my seatbelt together. I had a feeling that she was getting her mind right the way she leaned her head against the window and stared into the daylight of nowhere. We rode in silence for most of the trip. It seemed like it took me forever to the CMC emergency room, but it was actually only fifteen minutes. She slowly raised her head after discovering that we had been on our way to the hospital. I looked at her and she looked at me, neither of us saying a word.

Before we exited the vehicle, I felt the need to tell her the real reason why we were here. She deserved to at least know that it was concerning her husband.

"Look, Dee, before we go in here, there is something I need to tell you."

"Oh, there's no need. I guess you think bringing me here will force me to find out what's wrong with me. I told you that I was going to call Dr. Legare if I didn't feel well tomorrow. But, I see - "

"Dayna, Dayna! As much as I know you are in pain right now, our being here has nothing to do with you."

"Then, why are we here?" She tilted her head to the side waiting for me to explain myself.

"It's Braylon."

"Braylon?"

"Yes, Braylon."

"What does he have to do with the pain in my chest?" She doesn't get it, I thought.

"Mom called and told us to get here right away. That's all I know."

The valet met us at the emergency room bay with a wheelchair and a clipboard. I barely moved the shifter in gear before I jumped out and ran across the front of the jeep by the time the young man had reached for the door handle.

"Are you well enough to walk?" I reached for Dayna's purse as she wrapped her arm around my neck for added support.

"I'll be fine."

"Ma'am, are you sure?" The young man steadied the chair in the event she needed to be escorted.

"Yes. I am sure."

I draped both purses on my forearm, tossed the keys to the valet and steadied Dayna on my arm. "Walters!" I shouted over my shoulder as we made our way into the emergency room department to find out what was going on.

***

Nurse after nurse and hall after hall, we finally made our way to emergency room 5-C. The only thing the triage nurses would tell us was how to get to him; no one offered any more information than that.

Dayna paused for a moment before entering the room. We could see several silhouettes on the other side of the curtain.

Just then, the curtain slid open first to the left and then to the right. Two doctors walked away with a grimacing expression. One of the RNs remained.

Dayna covered her mouth and let out a screeching cry. Mom turned around just in time to see her buckling at the knees. I tried to help her from behind, but within two steps daddy was by our side embracing his oldest child.

Braylon lay anatomically connected to at least six different machines. Through the beeps and hollowed air compressions, the only other sounds we could hear were Dayna's sobs.

"Braylon! Braylon! Baby, what happened?" The attending RN looked in our direction. "Somebody please tell me what happened to my husband!" Her crying was becoming more uncontrollable so Daddy hugged her even tighter. We were all in tears.

The nurse stepped closer and offered each of us a cup of water before leading us to a private family consultation room.

"Excuse me, you are?"

"This is Mr. Walters' wife, Dayna Walters," I answered through my tears. "I'm his sister-in-law, Nevaeh and these are our parents, Sabrina and Lance Jones."

"Yes. We've met already. Please, have a seat." She guided us to one of the sofas. "Let me get Dr. Bazemore for you."

We all sat in silence as Dayna continued to cry hysterically. I did my best to calm her down. We all did, but nothing seemed to work.

Dr. Bazemore joined us after a while and we were finally met with the moment of truth. He explained how Braylon had come into the ER with multiple gunshot wounds and further explained how he was hit by several bullets in the chest, shoulder and left leg. He was listed in critical condition. Because of his injuries, he had lost several pints of blood, and thusly, had slipped into a coma.

As if the news that we just heard wasn't enough, none of us could have imagined what happened next. "Miss? Miss? Are you OK?" With her hand clutched across her chest, Dayna collapsed in the middle of the room, falling hard to the floor.

"I need 3 HBP units in here stat! We have a code blue!" The doctor yelled into his earpiece as he repositioned her and checked her pupils for signs of dilation.

Other medical officials came rushing in one after another. We watched in horror as one medic hooked my sister up to an oxygen machine while another one started an IV. Mom was hysterical and I was a nervous wreck. Daddy tried to remain strong for the both of us, but the stress on his face expressed that it was too much for him to bear.

Initially, we arrived at the hospital to find out what had happened to Braylon and we did. But, we also ended up staying at the hospital as my sister tried desperately to hold on to her precious life.

After six hours of waiting for an update on Dayna's condition, the doctor returned to tell us that she had had a massive heart attack. I decided that maybe I should go home to at least get a shower, get a change of clothes and grab my spare charger from the kitchen. I also needed to contact our business partners to let them know what was going on. And how could I forget to call Syn back.

Our mother requested that Dayna and Braylon be placed in the same room so if one of them woke up they would be able to see the other was still by their side.

There was nothing left to do at this point except to call on Him and hope that He hadn't forgotten about us, especially during a time like this because we needed Him now more than ever.

Chapter 21 - Chance

Monday morning came too soon. After making arrangements for a car service last night, I turned in shortly thereafter. I didn't get much sleep because I couldn't stop thinking about Nevaeh. She was absolutely perfect for me. There was nothing about her I would change – except for her last name. The reality set in not long after I saw her leaving yesterday that I didn't even know her last name. And for that sake and that sake alone, I hoped that Nevaeh was really her first name.

The ride to the airport had given me a little more time to think. I thought about my schedule for the upcoming week and what time management miracles I needed to implore. Thoughts about my business-turned-personal excursions on the Caribbean island provoked a secret smile within. That woman had me in the heart. I only hoped that she felt the same way.

Once, I landed at the airport back in the states, I immediately checked my voice messages. Of them five from my right hand man, Dr. Himes. There seemed to be a rash of emergencies that had come about at the medical center. There goes my plan for playing hooky and taking an extra day.

Before I was able to listen to the next message, an incoming call interrupted the voice command. It was Jennis.

"Doc. How are you? I was just listening to my messages and heard several from you. What's going on?"

"Dr. Mathis, we need you to get to the ER as soon as possible. There have been several critical situations that have come in. For one of the cases, we're not so sure he's going to make it."

"What's the situation?"

"GSW. Multiple. He was ambushed. There is also a cardiac case, and it's a rather strange one if you ask me. I've never seen anything like this before."

"You take the GSW until I arrive and put Dr. Fisher on the cardiac patient. I'm just leaving baggage claim. I should be there within the next thirty minutes."

"Figured you would say that. I'm already on it. I'll see you when you get here, sir."

I ended the call, grabbed my bags and hailed the nearest taxi. The driver for the Charlotte Airport Executive Transportation Service gestured towards me.

"Where to, sir. You look like you could be in a hurry."

"Your observation would be right. I need to get to Carolinas Medical stat."

"You got it!" The tires of the black SUV screeched as we weaved through traffic, practically breaking every traffic law known to mankind. Those laws were doubly broken because we were breaking them on the restricted grounds of the airport. I readied myself in the backseat, looping my neck with my stethoscope and replacing my jacket with my medical coat. I jotted a few notes down into my steno pad.

"How much longer?" I placed the book back into my carry on.

"We should be there within the next five minutes. I just need to get around this band of traffic."

"Great. Do what you have to do. I've got a feeling it's going to be a long night."

Well, well, well. What do we have here? I guess lightening does strike in the same place twice. A two for one special. LOL! I'm pitching a tent just thinking about the look on that bitch face when she found out what happened to her husband. I bet you she will think twice about the karma she puts in the air, especially if it falls on me. What the hell does she think I am? A joke? No one does to me what she did and thinks they can get away with it. Well, we'll see who gets the last laugh!

I can't believe my luck.

Now, let the games begin.

Signed,

One Pissed Off Black Man

Chapter 22 - Jennis

The madhouse this place has become was definitely one for the record books. Word had gotten out about the gunshot victim we had and the media has created friction in front of the hospital. It was everything I could do not to respond inappropriately to the situation, but some of the reporters were really pushing it. One of them managed to sneak past the guard at the end of the hallway and tried to enter the room to get a money shot. How low could one go?

I assigned Aimee, our director of media relations, to handle the situation by creating some damage control. Falsely, and under the advice of our staff attorney, we had to release a statement saying that our patient, Braylon Walters, was being treated for non-life threatening injuries and would soon be transported to the Wake County Medical Center for specialized treatment. The main thing was to move people away so as to not jeopardize the safety of our current patients or any patients that attempted to seek medical treatment at our facility.

Having someone like Braylon Walters, *the* attorney Braylon Walters, was on the same level as having to treat a mega celebrity from Hollywood during the height of their career. We received all kinds of phone calls from media outlets wanting to get an exclusive story, from women all over the country claiming to be his wife and the least of them, from men and women claiming that he was their long lost father. How desperate can some people be?

I grabbed my clip board and headed towards The Walters' room. When I arrived, I saw Dr. Fisher was already there.

"Doc. What's up, man? Yo, this dude right here got dealt wit'. Have you seen the size of these holes, man?"

"If you are attempting to assess his current situation, Dr. Fisher, I suggest you remember that this is a professional setting and your language and tone should be a precise reflection as such."

"Oh. My bad. I mean, I understand, Dr. Himes. You're right." He stepped closer to his monitor and adjusted a few dials before proceeding to give me an update on Mr. Walters' condition. He had a very unique way of evaluating and assessing patient conditions. It seemed like the more complex the condition was the more intricate his evaluation became. He was phenomenal... in that regard.

"Thank you. Let's continue to keep monitoring his status. This one's a priority case. We've been instructed to do everything possible to preserve his life and that's just what we'll do."

"Yes, Dr. Himes." He clicked a few more buttons and entered more data into the computer terminal. "OK. He's good to go. All medications have been administered and all monitors have been elevated for maximum observation.

Now, if you will excuse me, I have another patient to tend to."

"Sure. Thanks." I turned to walk out of the room. "Oh, and by the way. Dr. Mathis is on his way in; he should be here at any minute now. We've decided to move our staff meeting up to ten o'clock tonight instead of first thing in the morning. There are a number of cases that we need to be made aware of and Attorney Simmons needs to brief us on a legal matter. She said it was urgent and that all staff needed to be present."

"I'll be there, sir."

"Good job, Dr. Fisher. See you later tonight." I headed out into the hallway and made my way back to the office.

I sat down and thumbed through the standing files on my desk when I noticed a manila envelope across my keyboard. I moved the envelope to the side and began to review the contents of the Walters file. I was looking for anything in his medical history that would inform us of any past medical conditions that we needed to be aware of as his condition progressed. Usually, there would be some indication of a family history or ailments such as diabetes or cancer that would guide our treatment. Combining certain medications could prove to be more harmful than the condition in which a patient was currently in so we had to be careful.

I read a few more lines and made a few notes...and began to think.

Chapter 23 - Nevaeh

There simply wasn't enough time in the day. Between showers and phone calls I barely had enough time to think. I grabbed the overnight bag I packed, set the alarm and headed back to the hospital.

From the moment we got back from the islands, everything seemed to be one big blur and I couldn't get those images out of my head -- Dayna clinching her chest and falling over at the news of her husband's attack, and now she lay beside him, in the hospital, both fighting for their lives.

It took forever, but I was finally able to reach Syn after calling her all night and half the morning. She had been on a little rendezvous with God knows who and had finally picked up her phone. Since she was already out and about, she was planning to meet me at the hospital later this afternoon. Mom and Dad were going to come a little later as well.

Parking was a nightmare as usual and my nerves couldn't take another setback. The closest space I could find was on the eighth level.

The patient information receptionist at the nurse's station greeted me as I made my way into Mecklenberg Tower. She provided directions on the best way to locate my sister's room, using one of the hospital maps to emphasize her instructions. I looked at the map and thanked her for her time.

She looked around me just as I was about to walk off. "Oh, Dr. Mathis. Wait. This message came in for you." She retrieved a piece of paper from a large paper clip holder near her computer screen.

"Hey, Nurse Ashley! Thank you for – Nevaeh?"

I turned around to see Chance standing next to me. He was dressed in a long, white lab coat with a stethoscope comforting his neck. The embroidery on his left lapel said **Dr. Chancellor Mathis, M.D. Executive Director of the Traumatic Center.**

"Chance?"

"Oh, my God!" *My prayers have been answered!* He grabbed me and hugged me tightly, his clip board pressing flat against my back. "Nevaeh, what are you doing here? I thought I would never see you again. I was going to contact Queen Latifah, Steve Harvey or somebody to do a reunion show just for me!" His excitement radiantly beamed. All the nurses at the station stopped what they were doing and turned to look at us. Many of them smiling at the comments they had overheard. He stepped back and took a long look at me. He noticed the drab expression I had on my face and suddenly shifted his demeanor.

"Hello, Chance. Or shall I say, Dr. Mathis." I nodded towards his jacket.

"Yes, it's Dr. Mathis. What are you doing here?"

I heard him the first time, but tried to avoid answering him. His inquiry hit home as it reminded me of the very reason why I was here. One of the joys of my life lay helplessly and there wasn't anything I can do but wait. But, I would wait for her. Pray for her.

"It's -. It's –"

"Come with me. Let's talk in here." He grabbed my hand.

"No, I can't. It's my sister. Dayna. Her husband was admitted to the hospital the other day, suffering from multiple gunshot wounds. When the nurses broke the news to her, she collapsed and slipped into a coma. They're both in a coma. I just came here to pray for my sister and my brother-in-law." I tried my best to be strong, especially in front of him and the hospital staff, but my feelings had gotten the best of me as the tears of burden and uncertainty began to flow from the corners of my eyes.

"Oh, baby. I'm sorry. I'm so sorry to hear about your family." He gently embraced me. "Please. Is there anything I can do to help?"

"Yes. Pray for them. Pray for us, please."

"Consider it done." He soothed my back in a circular motion. "May I walk with you to her room?"

He grabbed a tissue from the front desk and dabbed my eyes. "Sure, if you'd like. She's in room 1345." He checked one last time to make sure he had gotten each drop of salt water from my face.

"I know the way. This way, please." I followed his guiding arm.

As we walked towards the room, three quick beeps interrupted the sound of our footsteps. I noticed he didn't bother to reach for it right away, mainly because we were stepping onto the elevator. He pressed the button to take us to the thirteenth floor.

We stood just outside of room 1345. I reached into my purse to lower the volume on my phone. When I did, I noticed I had missed a couple of text messages. One was from Syn and the other was from Sydney. I swiped the screen to lock it back and tapped on the door.

I pushed the door slightly, carefully entering the solace of her hospital room.

I wasn't prepared to see what I saw and had I not seen it with my own eyes I would have thought I was dreaming.

A man dressed in medical scrubs stood over Dayna on top of her bed. He was holding his penis in his hands, moving back and forth urinating on top of her. His human discharge tye-dyed the linen that covered her. Drops of his golden shower dribbled down the sides of her face, trickled over her lips, and stained the pillow beneath her head.

"What the hell?" Chance raced in and yanked the man from the bed. He threw him down and tried to hold him there, but it was too late. The man had somehow maneuvered his way out of his grip, flipped him over and Chance went crashing into the mirrored closet door. I managed to move out of the way just in time and scooted on the other side of the bed, positioning myself between Dayna and Braylon. I screamed for someone to call for security hoping someone in the hallway heard me.

Chance squared off on him. The man went to charge him in a tackling manner and Chance stopped him with a one-two combo. He staggered and aimed at Chance again. This time, he swung and the blow connected on the left side of Chance's face. The strike was dismissed as he popped him one good one square on the chin knocking the man out of the room and into the hallway. The gaping sized hole in the wall told the whole story.

Moments later, the hallway and the room were swarming with security officials. Other doctors and nurses came rushing to the doctor's aid while two guards pinned the unknown man down. Seconds later a few city police officers came rushing in.

One of the nurses bombarded her way through the commotion after noticing that Dayna's vital monitor was beeping wildly.

"Dear God!" She looked in fear at the display as she saw the indication of how high Dayna's heart rate had gotten. "Hurry! Get in here, quick! We need to rush three CC's of naloxone, stat! This woman's heart is about to explode!"

***

By the time Syn had arrived, there had been a beat down, an arrest, and a life saved, all within twenty minutes, while Dayna and Braylon rest peacefully through it all. After I was finally able to collect myself, I told her everything that went down. In usual fashion, she was ready to set it off. She started cursing and ranting all over the waiting room. I tried to shut her up as fast as I could, but I wasn't as successful as I'd hoped.

"Delanie Synatra Jones, you watch your mouth!" Mother was standing right behind her with our father at her side. "I can hear you all the way down the hall. What's the matter with you, girl?"

"I'm sorry, mom, but you don't understand."

"I understand your using all that foul language is not going to take care of whatever it is that has you so upset!" Mom put her purse down next to me and placed her hands on her hips. Dad walked closer.

"Sabrina, calm down. In fact, both of you calm down." He stood between them like a referee giving orders to each fighter at a boxing match. "Sit down, Synatra, and tell us what's going on."

She looked at him sideways, not saying a word. With arms folded, she crossed her legs and bounced her foot up and down.

"Synatra. I'm waiting." Mom took a seat next to her and dad followed suit.

"Dad, let me." I placed my hand across Synatra's arm and looked at her, looking for some support as I was about to share the chaos that had transpired.

I opened my mouth and began to tell them word for word, and action for action about what happened on the thirteenth floor. Hearing the news made mother very upset. Dad's feelings and emotions were equally wounded.

It was all that either one of us could do to not go and snatch a knot into that guy. The longer mother thought about what happened to her oldest baby, she cried something awful. Dad did his best to comfort her, but it was rather difficult for him to do between bugging out his eyes and raising his voice at the news of what happened.

We sat in the waiting room for the next three hours, praying and comforting one another. Dad had managed to calm down – slightly. The hospital staff wouldn't allow us back in the room since it was now considered a crime scene, so we decided to sit there and wait until they did.

One of the nurses on staff had come to tell us that we wouldn't be allowed to go back in the room any more until the room was cleared for visitors. There were too many reports that needed to get completed and they were afraid that with all of the commotion both Dayna and Braylon would somehow have an adverse effect to the treatment they were receiving. Although unconscious, their subconscious was still able to detect danger and fear, thus causing undue stress and tension on the brain. We didn't want to contribute to any of these factors, so we all decided that waiting at home would be what was best.

One by one we filed out of the waiting room and headed to our respective vehicles. We hugged each other mightily before departing from the parking deck.

Both Synatra and Dad still wore looks that could kill. I worried about them.

I said a special prayer for my family, hoping that God would answer it and answer it suddenly. I hooked my phone up to the charger, set my mp3 player to my gospel playlist and headed for the house.

Chapter 24 ~ Chance

"Will somebody please tell me what the hell is going on?" I had never seen Dr. Himes like this before. He was pacing back and forth across the floor in the conference room. "What is this? Fighting? Cursing and screaming? And, did I hear something about someone urinating on a patient?"

No one in the room said a word, including me. I repositioned the bag of ice on my hand, trying to calm down further.

Nia sat silently looking around at everyone as if to say that she didn't know nothing, hadn't seen nothing and wasn't in the business of learning about nothing that didn't deal with her. Instead, she scrolled through a few twitter feeds and minded her own business. A few of the other physicians sat dumbfounded. Some of them had heard about what went down through the company instant messaging system. Once one person found out they shared it with another and then another with another and so on. One of my aunts used to always say that there were only three types of communication devices - 'telephone, telegram and tell a ninja'.

There was no doubt that the fact that I had gotten into a physical altercation with a fellow colleague was on the tip of what everyone was thinking. I was busy trying to figure this all out myself. What I couldn't wrap my mind around was why Dr. Fisher would behave in such an unbecoming and unprofessional manner. He took it way too far. That kind of behavior was criminal and grounds for having your medical license revoked, never to be reinstated. It just didn't make sense why he would do something like that. He was on the cusp of receiving the medical innovation of the year award from the medical alliance of health care management for the state. The awards ceremony was scheduled for next month and it was a big to-do. Rest assured, his time as a physician in my hospital was over.

Sure I thought about the incident that had occurred, but I also thought about my run in with luck. My blessing out of all of this was that I had run into the woman with whom I had shared the perfect night with – the woman whom I thought I would never see again – only to find out that her sister was a comatose patient in *my* hospital. I still wondered what they were doing in Charlotte.

Just as my mind was traveling to a happier place, Attorney Simmons walked in carrying a file as thick as a PDR. The room was still soundless while we all focused our attention on the set-up Simmons was making on the round table in the corner of the room.

Finally, feeling the need to slice through the tension in the air, I said "Look. Let me update everyone on what has taken place."

"No, please allow me," Attorney Simmons interjected. "But, before I do, I need to ask for everyone to leave except for Drs. Mathis and Himes," then she turned to her left and said "and you, Nia. I need for the three of you to stay. Everyone else, you are dismissed." Those whose names were not called stood and exited the room. Some of them mumbled a thing or two but none of it was audible.

"Lady, and gentlemen, there are a few things you need to know regarding the reasons I have asked you all to stay. As you may or may not know there has been talk for several months now about the economy and the impact it has had on the medical center." I sat motionless while she continued. "Now, despite everything that has taken place, I think you need to know that I saw this coming. Not this particular incident, but I knew it was only a matter of time before we would have to downsize our staff."

We all turned and looked at one another, wondering if one or all of us was about to get the ax. I didn't quite understand why she asked the three of us to remain, but I trusted her judgment and knew that there was a method to the madness.

"Dr. Mathis, I have asked you to stay because as executive director of this facility, you need to be brought up to speed on what we're up against." She walked closer to the table next to Jennis. "Because of your position, Dr. Himes, you have been asked to stay as your position entitles you to the privileged information I am about to share. As second in command, you are just as accountable as Dr. Mathis.

"So, that leaves you, Nia." The smile she gave her displayed a hint of satisfaction and like in her gesture which wasn't her usual demeanor. "You, my friend, get the award for best assistant ever." Nia quickly looked up from her phone and then at each of us, clearly at a loss for words. She looked around the room like she was waiting for a camera crew to come running from the hallway yelling 'psych'.

"I'll take your quietness as an invitation to further explain."

She tossed each of us a manila envelope that contained some pretty classified documents. She kept a few papers to herself. To my surprise, in fact to all of our surprise, there lying before us were copies of police reports, tax documents, personnel documents, education records, photos, you name it. They all belonged to none other than Christopher Hamilton Fisher.

Page after page revealed some pretty nasty truths, truths that he had not disclosed upon his hiring. His educational background report revealed that he only completed an online course in accounting at the community college level. Copies of the police reports exposed him for being wanted for embezzlement and defrauding the federal government back in Detroit. He also had two warrants for his arrest from Greensboro and Climax, NC for grand theft larceny and suspicions of identity theft, respectively. But, the one truth that showed on this paperwork as the biggest lie was the fact that he was not a licensed medical doctor.

On his application he noted that his degree was conferred at UNC-Chapel Hill. He had forged his transcripts and the actual degree. I couldn't believe it. Dr. Himes shuffled through the documents like a deck of cards. He seemed more and more amazed the more he read. Nia, on the other hand, went back to Facebooking after she briefly reviewed the contents.

"This, um, this is unbelievable. How did you find all of this? What prompted your research?" I pushed the envelope away from me, leaned back and crossed my legs.

She gave me the look that she had given Nia earlier. "Oh, no, Dr. Mathis. I didn't discover all of this by myself. You have Ms. Nia to thank as well, but not for the information you have just received. Be sure to thank her for this." She placed a sheet of paper face down in front of us one by one. "Now, turn it over."

As if the truth that was just revealed wasn't enough, this absolutely took the cake. I held in my hands a picture of a man dressed in hospital issued scrubs, carrying a medium-sized duffle bag. The other images were of different angles produced from a surveillance camera that showed a clear appearance of the man of the hour, Christopher Hamilton Fisher.

The most shocking thing wasn't that he was carrying a duffle bag. No. It was unzipped. The camera nearest the parking garage captured the likeness of a tiny face with a head full of hair.

That fool had stolen a baby.

I was done. I was completely outdone with the competition of this news versus my right mind because at this moment I couldn't think straight to save my life and that almost never happens. From the look on his face, Dr. Himes was just as perplexed as I was. But Nia, on the other hand, continued to sit without making a sound.

Chapter 25 - Nia

Finally. Attorney Simmons had dropped the bomb on the good doctors. I really wanted to think that all of this was some kind of sick joke someone was playing on Dr., no Chris Fisher, but it wasn't.

As she revealed her hand, I didn't say a word. I just kept on scrolling through my Facebook page reading updates and looking at pictures. I felt like I had said enough by sharing my findings with Simmons.

When Marlena Simmons first arrived I liked her from the moment she stepped in the office. She was a sharp sister, both intellectually and personally. She came to us fresh out of law school, but the way in which she carried herself, one would have thought that she had practiced law for at least twenty years. She had the kind of intellect that often produced ah-ha moments and raised the bar on critical thinking skills. She was the kind of thought leader that could separate the haves from the have nots of business acumen. Some had it, others didn't.

Marlena had a lot of business connections with whom she networked while in law school. She had inside tracks with the media, other lawyers and medical professionals, and some of the local non-profit organizations. Hell, she even had connections in politics and the school systems. It was of no surprise to me that she had won numerous awards for her legal expertise and her volunteer contributions to society. She was as 'they' say a bad mamma-jamma.

I noticed Dr. Mathis looking at me the whole time he was examining the paperwork. I was trying to figure out what he could have been thinking. I just hoped he wasn't thinking that my silence was an indication that I had something to do with any of the fraud's wrongdoings. But, as he sat upright and clasped his hands together it appeared as if I was about to find out.

"Nia. I want to ask you something." I paid closer attention. "It doesn't matter what your answer is as long as it is the truth, OK?"

"Yes, Dr. Mathis."

"What, if any, do you have to do with any of this?"

I looked at Attorney Simmons, who was just now taking a seat, and then over to Dr. Himes for a reaction. I didn't receive anything from either.

"Well, Dr. Mathis. Let me start off by saying that I value my employment here and just as equally, I value the relationships I have built with our customers and the staff. But, more importantly I am humbly honored by the many lessons and invaluable professional development I have received from working with two – I mean three – fine professionals such as yourselves. But to answer your question, I didn't have anything to do with any of the transgressions of Dr. Fisher."

"Chris."

"Yes, Chris. Thank you, sir." I asserted my position a bit further. "But, there is one thing I do wish to share with you in terms of answering your question. I want to share with you how I came upon these misleadings."

I began by telling the ad hoc committee of my close relationship with my cousin, Felicity, and how she had never known who her real father was. One day while I was being entertained by the many minions on the Book, I came across a post where a follower was searching for a missing loved one so I decided to click on the link.

There were thousands of people looking for long lost family members and friends. Many of the posts were sons and daughters. Some of them had discovered family photos that prompted them to question why they didn't look like everyone else. Others had simply found out – mostly the hard way – that they were adopted and decided to look for their birth mother or father.

One post in particular struck me as odd. It contained a link to another page where law enforcement agencies would post images associated with unsolved cases so I checked it out. The very first picture that I came across I recognized the man that was walking out carrying that duffle bag with a baby inside. Sure, the man had hair on his head at the time, but I quickly recognized him as being none other than Chris Fisher.

I did a little more research through numerous search engines and social media sites and discovered the material that we just reviewed and told Marlena about it and she took it from there.

THE SIDE EFFECTS OF LOVE

"I gave the information to you a few weeks ago before you left for your conference, Dr. Mathis." He said nothing so I directed my next revelation towards Dr. Himes. "When I didn't hear back from him, I slipped a copy on your chair the other day, hoping you would get it and go to doc with it." I waited for a response from Dr. Himes, but all he did was shake his head as he remembered the envelope that he tossed on his desk after receiving a phone call.

"Dang! Here I was thinking you had no personality, no means of ever coming out of that shell in which you appeared to find comfort, but I am pleased to admit that I couldn't have been more wrong. Good work, Ms. Anderson. Good work!" Dr. Himes politely gave me a pat on the back.

"Thanks, Dr. Himes, but with all due respect, never underestimate the power of an introvert."

Dr. Mathis, on the other hand, still had a scowl look on his face. He was clearly livid about what had gone down. He put his hands in his pocket as he stood.

"Attorney Simmons, I want this man removed from the premises in all facets not now but right now. He is a disgrace to the medical profession, this hospital, and to this team. He has to go. And, yes, I am pressing full charges." With that he turned and left the conference room.

Chapter 26 - Nevaeh

What a night. As soon as I walked through the door, I disrobed, took a long, hot shower and crawled in the bed. All of my energy had vacated my body so I did the only thing I knew how to do: regain my strength through the reading of the Word and then call it a night.

Just as I had finished my nightly lesson, my phone rang. I saw that it was just after eleven so I wondered who would be calling me at this time of night.

I didn't recognize the number on the screen, but I thought it was best that I answered it just in case someone from the hospital was calling with an update about Dayna or Braylon.

"Hello?" My voice was just as tired and sleepy as I was.

"Nevaeh?"

"Yes? Who is this?"

"It's Chance, Nevaeh." A moment of calm thickened the air.

"Chance?"

"Yes."

"Chance. How did you get my number?"

"I'm a bit embarrassed to say, but I actually got your number from your sister's file. I believe you were listed as one of her emergency contacts."

"So, you stole my number is what you're telling me?"

"Not quite. More like seized an opportunity to take advantage of my position and the resources that are provided because of it."

"Oh, see now you're just trying to be cute!" As much as I hated to admit it, the little laughter that did escape my soul was welcomed. "What can I do for you? Is something wrong with Dayna? Braylon?"

"No, no. It's nothing like that. I wanted to call to check on you to see how you were holding up. I didn't wake you, did I?"

Suddenly, my weariness had vanished as I listened more intensely. "Thank you for thinking of me."

"You're very welcome. What's that I hear in your voice? Are you blushing?"

"Something like that. I'm wearing the smile that you have given me." *I'm blushing. Big time!*

We talked for another hour or so before my eyelids began to close and I began to check my eyes for cracks.

***

Early the next morning, I was awakened by the sound of my alarm which meant that it was already six o'clock.

After washing my face and brushing my teeth I decided to catch up on a little bit of email before going to pick up mom. We had planned on returning to the hospital to check on the status of things so I wanted to kill some time before heading out.

Sydney had kept me abreast of everything that had taken place during my absence, which was now going on two weeks. I clicked on one of the emails and noticed that she had secured a contract with a medical center to do some assessment on their personnel and human resource management for their staff. I was even more pleased that the contract was stacked upwards of thirty-six thousand dollars. After sending her a message to take care of everything and keep me updated, I got dressed and headed towards my folks place.

The traffic on 85 was moving at a snail's pace as usual, thus giving Mom and me some additional time to talk and catch up on things. She spoke about her concerns of her oldest and her son-in-law and how none of what had taken place made much sense to her. She went in her purse and pulled out her bible and clutched it tightly as she prayed for them. The radio was reporting that there was an overturned big rig a few exits ahead of us, so the next chance I got, I detoured from the congestion and took a few back roads.

After parking, we made our way back to the not-so-lucky thirteenth floor. Thankfully, one of the nurses that was there the other night was there again this morning. She remembered us and immediately went to grab a doctor to give us clearance to enter the room.

Shortly after her summons, one of the doctors from the trauma unit greeted us in the foyer of the critical care unit.

"Good morning, ladies. My name is Dr. Jennis Himes. Pleased to meet you." We exchanged pleasantries. "So, I know why you are here so I won't prolong what I have to say. May we please step into a private room? After the briefing, we will get you inside to see your loved ones." We followed him into a smaller, quaint room and both took a seat.

No sooner had our butts hit the seat, Mom immediately went into a word of prayer. Dr. Himes and I patiently waited. She took a deep breath, raised her head and said, "OK, doctor. What's going on with my babies?"

"Mrs. Jones, Ms. Jones, what I am about to say is not easy for me by no stretch of the imagination. If at any time you have any questions, please do not hesitate to stop me and ask. Let's start with your son-in-law, first. As you know, Mr. Walters has been admitted after suffering from multiple gunshot wounds."

"Define multiple." Mom pursed her lips and braced herself for the answer.

"Nine." She lowered her head and shook it. "Five of them struck him in some pretty critical places, but the one we are most concerned with is the one that is lodged near his heart."

"His heart!" I gasped for air.

"Yes, his heart."

I removed my hand from my mouth and wondered, "Is there anything that can be done to remove it? Surgery, perhaps?"

Calmly, Dr. Himes responded, "Well, that's just the thing. We can't perform surgery on this type of injury."

"I don't understand." Mom and I looked at each other.

"The way the bullet is positioned, it's lodged right against the wall of his heart, his swollen heart. If his heart continues to swell it will only tighten the area around it making it that much more difficult to access the bullet. Surgery will intensify the swelling and that's not what we want. The other side to that is that the bullet is working against him right now and, it's not looking too good for him."

"So, what you're saying is…?"

"We are in a catch 22 position. We can't remove it because it's too risky and we can't leave it in there because it's putting his life in more danger."

"So, what do we do?"

"We have to take a chance and wait. Waiting is the best option we have right now, despite the circumstances. That, and prayer."

A streak of quietness hung in the air while we absorbed what we had just been told.

Mom grabbed a tissue from her purse and dabbed at the corners of her eyes. "What about Dayna? What's going on with her?" Our answer was interrupted by a knock at the door. Synatra walked in looking exhausted.

"Hey everybody." Mom and I stood to hug her.

"Dr. Himes, this is our baby sister, Synatra." He reached over to shake her hand. "You're just in time, baby girl. Dr. Himes was about to update us on Dayna's condition." I supported her back as she took her seat.

"Dayna's condition is a bit complicated, yet interesting at the same time. We initially thought it was a heart attack, but what we discovered was that she is suffering from a severe case of stress cardiomyopathy. In other words, she has a broken heart. My guess would be that with the news and the grief of what happened to her husband she experienced an aggressive rush of adrenaline and other chemicals of the body which left her heart unable to pump properly which led to her current state.

"Although she's in a coma, please know that she's going to be touch and go for a while, but she is stable. Right now we are treating her with a moderate dose of anti-anxiety medications and some pain medicine."

Synatra asked, "Can we see them?"

"Sure, sure. You can see them for a little while, but not much longer than that. They both really need their rest so I'd only ask you to keep it brief. I'll give you ladies a few moments of privacy. I'll be waiting for you in the hallway."

He stood and left the room, leaving us to stew in the updates we just received.

Chapter 27 - Chance

I needed a moment to clear my head after the meeting with Simmons and Himes. The fact that this guy had worked under me for all these years as a fraud just didn't sit well with me. Just because I had inherited this team from my predecessor didn't mean that I should have been this lax in my leadership.

I walked up to the nurse's station to follow up on a patient. I noticed Dr. Himes standing in the hallway so I made my way over to him.

"Doc. How are you holding up?"

"I'm good, sir. Just grabbing this file for review and follow up. What's your position?"

"Well, I just finished meeting with the Walters family. I briefed them on the current situation of both patients based on the initial report."

"The married couple on the thirteenth floor?"

"Yes, that's the one."

"Oh. That's the case I was looking into. Mind if I join you?"

"No, no. Not at all." The door to the meeting room opened and a woman with a short, salt and pepper cut stepped out first, followed by a young lady that was clearly upset. "Ah, Mrs. Jones. Young lady. Is everything OK? Where is uh, uh…"

"Nevaeh," the motherly woman completed.

"Yes, Nevaeh. Forgive me. I'm a little bad with names."

"She'll be out in a moment. She's finishing a phone call."

Dr. Himes introduced me to the family and we conversed for a bit while waiting for the other member of their family to join us. Somehow just the thought of her being near me brought a certain calmness to my spirit.

She stepped into the hallway just as I was checking my communicator for a message that I had just received. She was looking into her purse when she bumped into me.

"Chance! Hello, again!"

"Hello, Ms. Jones. Pleasure to see you again. Hopefully this visit will be more pleasant than the last."

"I should hope so." She grabbed the hand of whom I assumed to be her mother. "Shall we go?"

"You two know each other?" Dr. Himes asked as he pointed between the both of us.

"Something like that. Ms. Jones and I met earlier this week," I responded all the while watching at her.

"Oh, OK. Well, Jones family, if you would follow me right this way, please." We all followed him as he led us back to the room.

***

Mr. and Mrs. Walters lay peacefully with one another. No one said a word. The younger member began to cry, falling into Nevaeh's arms. The "mother" stood silently.

"All, I hate to do this here," I explained, "but I need to ask you a few questions about Mrs. Walters. Would that be OK?"

Nevaeh responded, "Sure. What would you like to know?"

"Does she have a history of heart problems?"

"No. Not that I am aware. Mom?" She looked in her direction, seeking any answers she may have had.

"No. I don't know of anything going on with her either."

"Well, according to our records, she experienced something very similar to this about twenty years back and even then, she remained hospitalized for about a week and a half." I noticed the puzzled looks on everyone's face as I flipped through a few more documents. "Does any of this ring a bell?"

"Twenty years ago? What you mean twenty years ago?"

"I'm sorry, you are?"

"My name is Synatra and that's my big sister."

"I'm sorry to startle you with this information, Synatra, but her records indicate that she has been dealing with a weak heart for quite some time now. It's very unfortunate, her condition, but I can assure you that my staff and I are going to do everything we can to save her and Mr. Walters, too. Which brings me to my next point.

"After the disturbance earlier in the week, we ran some tests to be sure that we hadn't missed anything and also to determine if her assailant had tampered with her medication."

Mother Jones said, "Go on."

"Yes, Mrs. Jones. What we found was that she had an elevated level of pain medication in her system. Apparently, she was injected with four times the legal limit of an experimental, new age painkiller. Luckily, one of the responding nurses caught it in time to reverse the effects before any harm or permanent damage could be done."

"Who is this person? What is being done about this? Why would he do this to my baby?" Mother Jones's questions riddled off one by one as she began to cry. Nevaeh attempted to calm her down again.

"Mrs. Jones, please know that we are doing everything we can to get to the bottom of this." I looked at Jennis for confirmation.

"Yes, I concur, Mrs. Jones. We will conduct a full investigation in concert with our attorney and the Charlotte-Mecklenburg Police Department. You have my word on that."

I looked at Nevaeh and noticed that she had a look of mystery in her eyes. She never took her eyes off of her sister and I never took my eyes off of her.

Chapter 28 - Sabrina

Something didn't quite add up. Twenty years ago, Dayna was in her senior year of college. The entire time she was there, I don't recall anything about her having been hospitalized for a week. If anyone knew anything, I would bet my retirement savings that those two sisters of hers knew something. A mother knew her children and if it was one thing they knew about *me* was that I lived by one of many principles: what's done in the dark will always come to the light. A little birdie once told me that.

The ride back to the house was a quiet one. The only thing that was loud were the thoughts in my head. I suspected that they were both thinking about what they'd just heard and what lie they would concoct to try to cover for their oldest sister. That wasn't the usual M.O. for Nevaeh. She was kind of quiet, conservative and reserved. She carried herself with an heir of integrity that was unmatched, even with the best of them. But, that Synatra? Huh. She had always been full of surprises and could lay it on thick. She would connive and deceive to get whatever she wanted, so I didn't see why this situation would prove to be any different.

When we got in the house, Lance was standing at the kitchen counter slicing a piece of pound cake. I slammed my purse on the sofa table and went into the kitchen to fix me something to drink. The beverage pickings were pretty slim so I settled for orange juice even though it was no match for what I really wanted.

Lance didn't say anything. Yet, he looked to the girls for clues about what was going on. Neither of them returned his gaze so he transitioned into the living room and took a seat in his recliner.

Synatra sat nearest the door while Nevaeh went down the hallway towards the restroom. After a few minutes she came out and said, "Doesn't anybody have anything to say about what we just heard?"

"I was hoping you would do just that!" I agreed as I walked towards the hallway where she was standing. "Talk to me. Tell me something, because I want to know what's going on!"

"Mom, I don't know anything about anything. I promise. I am just as surprised as you." The confused look on Vay's face told me she was telling the truth.

Synatra jumped up from the sofa and came near the meeting location and said "Well, what I want to know is, who is this dude that attacked her like that? I mean, what the hell!" she chimed in.

"Synatra!"

"Sorry, Momma!"

Just then, the family patriarch interrupted and asked, "Is someone going to tell *me* what's going on?" No one made a sound. Not even me.

He sat upright in his chair. "I'm waiting." Having that man waiting was not a very smart thing to do. He could be extremely stubborn, not to mention downright impatient. But, before I moved to say anything about anything, I needed to make sure I at least knew what I was talking about. It wasn't enough for him to hear an I-don't-know response because you had better be able to tell him something. Not knowing just didn't quite cut it for him.

Nevaeh began to tell her father what we had learned at the hospital. He seemed taken aback by the news as well. He sat in silence and listened intently as each fact spewed from her mouth. No sooner had she finished, he stood and went into the bedroom and slammed the door.

Seizing a moment, I whispered to the girls, "Look, I think y'all need to leave now. Let me talk to him. Your daddy is very upset and I don't want y'all here when he comes back out of that room, you hear? Let me handle it."

"Yes, ma'am," they said in unison and headed for the door.

"Hold up, Vay. All of this who did it and why did they do it is making me sick to my stomach. Let me go use it before we leave, girl." Synatra fast-walked it to the bathroom. "Don't make no damn sense to me" she continued to rant.

Nevaeh didn't say another word. She went outside and sat in the jeep and waited.

As soon as Synatra left, I prepared myself for the barrage of questions that was about to consume this household. I looked to the heavens, locked the front door and headed for the bedroom.

Chapter 29 - Lance

The Lord don't make no mistakes. That's what my momma always told me. But, what about me? What about the mistakes I have made. My oldest baby girl was in the hospital fighting for her life. My son-in-law had been shot up and was struggling to live. My wife was about to have a fit because she wanted answers that no one was able to give her, and my other two babies were besieged with covert suspicions. And, here I was – standing in the need of prayer.

While Sabrina and the girls were in the front room, I sat on the side of the bed and prayed. The truth of the matter was it was too little and too late to pray now because what was done was done. I knew that one day the closet that held my secrets was going to come crashing open. It was only a matter of time.

As I prepared my soul to face the consequences of my decisions, I heard footsteps coming down the hallway. The door flew open revealing a very pissed off wife of mine. She leaned against the doorframe, not saying a word. She just looked at me. And looked at me. And looked at me. All men knew that when a woman was silent, she was thinking. It wasn't her thinking that was the problem. Not knowing *what* she was thinking was.

I'm all man, make no mistake about it, but I was scared as hell. My emotions were getting the best of me at the moment and I didn't know how to handle them. My heart beat pounded profusely and my skin moistened from the tension. I wasn't about to be the one to say anything first; I reserved that platform for her. That way, I could listen – or pretend to listen – giving me more time to think.

The perspiration from my forehead was beginning to run down the side of my face and I didn't even bother to wipe it off because I couldn't move. I couldn't think, and I definitely couldn't speak. Oh, what I would give to be somewhere else right now.

"Lance Adam Jones the third, do you love me?"

That did it. Now, she was trying to play with my head, playing these mind games and all. Twenty-five years we've been together and she hits me with a dumb question like that. What did she mean 'did I love her'? Of course I loved her. I shortened my internal conversation and answered, "Yes, sweetheart. Of course I love you. You know I do. Why would you ask me a silly thing like that?"

"Because I know you have questions, honey, and I know you don't like to hear the words 'I don't know'. In this household and as a part of our family creed, we value honesty, respect and communication. You know I would never lie to you, baby. I never have and I never will. But, if you want me to be honest with you, as I have been for the past twenty-five years, I honestly don't know anything about these heart issues Dayna has been having."

The Lord is good! Won't he do it?

Here I was thinking that my tomb of the unknown truth was about to be unearthed and she was clearly digging into something else. I breathed a short sigh of relief, setting the stage for my Oscar-winning performance.

"Oh, Sabby. Honey. Darling. Sweetheart, come here." I welcomed her with open arms as she walked towards me. "Listen to me, baby. Sure, I have questions and I am sure you do, too. We both want to know what is going on with our little girl, but we are in this together and we are going to get through this together. Alright?"

"Yes, dear. Thank you for understanding." She gave me one of those school-girl smiles she always wore whenever she got her way.

"Of course, love. Remember what I said – we are going to get through this together, OK?" She nodded her head in agreement. "Now, do you think I might be able to take my lovely wife out to lunch?"

"Why, yes I do!"

"Good. I think we could use a little time to settle ourselves from all that has happened. Then, afterwards we can go back to the hospital and check on baby girl." She smiled and I leaned down and hugged her womanly frame. While her shoulder was pressed against my chest, I lifted my head and thanked the Lord for making a way out of no way – one more time.

Now, let's see Denzel top that!

Chapter 30 - Nevaeh

"Sis, you mind taking me to the restaurant? I need to check on the numbers with Rosalyn." Synatra was still feeling some type of way about the whole day and the day was just getting started.

"Are you coming out to the hospital later?

"Fa show."

At Synatra's request, I took her back to the restaurant. Once I dropped her off, I figured I may as well stop by my office before heading back to the hospital.

Everything seemed to be running like a well-oiled machine. There were a few clients waiting to meet with our officers. As I walked down the hallway towards my office, I could hear a line of laughter coming from the break room area. There was a group of assistants in there gathered around a cell phone. I walked in front of the door when one of them spotted me, and hurriedly walked away from the others. Seeing the displeasure on my face made all of the laughter cease and everyone dispersed accordingly.

"Nevaeh! Oh, sweetie, it's so good to see you. How are you holding up?" Sydney greeted with a warm hug and a genuine smile as I entered my business quarters.

"I'm doing OK. Thanks for asking."

"Good. We just finished discussing that new contract I was telling you about."

"Oh. Then that explains why all of the support staff was caught slipping."

"Slipping? What do you mean?"

"Never mind. Tell me more about this contract everyone is buzzing about."

"You sure you're up for this? I mean, with your just returning to the office and all?"

"I'll be OK. Besides, I'm not going to be here long anyway. I just came to get an update, grab a few things and then I've got to head back over to the hospital."

Sydney began to outline the particulars of the CMC contract. I was half listening to her and half thinking about what could have been going on with my sister. I heard everything that Chance – Dr. Mathis – said in that room, as did everyone else, but what I couldn't come to terms with was the fact that Dayna hadn't told me about any of it. As close as we were, I truly didn't think that my sister would hold such a huge secret from me. Selfishly, it made me wonder what else she could be hiding from me.

To know that she has been suffering for so long sparked an anger in my soul. Is her condition something that can be cured? What if there is something going on with her that was going on with everyone? Do I need to make an appointment for an echocardiogram and get tested? This couldn't be happening. This just couldn't be happening.

"Ms. Jones? Are you OK?"

I was suddenly removed from my thoughts and brought back to the office. "Huh?"

"I said, 'are you ok'? You seemed to have tuned out for a bit."

"Oh. Um, yes, I'm fine," I lied.

"So, what do you think?"

"What do I think about what?"

"The contract with Carolinas Medical Center. Have you been listening to me?"

"Carolinas Medical Center? That's who this contract is with?"

"Yes."

"Who's the PI?"

"The Senior Executive Director for the Trauma Center, Dr. Chancellor Mathis."

"Chance?" The stunned look on my face revealed that I hadn't been listening after all. Sydney didn't respond so I said, "Who else is on this case from this side and theirs?"

"Well, I've been working with Arielle, Deacon and Kennedy from our team, and with a Dr. Jennis Himes and their attorney Marlena Simmons from the center."

"Good. I want you to take full control of this process. Make sure we are superb in our management of this contract. No slip ups. No mishaps. Nothing but excellence, alright? I want everything done that lies north of their expectations."

"Consider it done."

"I have faith and all the confidence in the world in your abilities. And just one more thing, I need you to hold down the fort for a while, at least for another week, OK?"

"Got it." Sydney re-assembled the file as she prepared to leave the room.

I stood to escort her to the door. "Thanks for everything, Syd. I owe you." We hugged and she left.

***

There had been no change in either of them. One of the nurses informed me that they would come in to turn him every six hours to prevent bed sores from forming, but that Braylon's condition was worsening because of that bullet and Dayna's condition remained the same, however her vitals were stable.

With Dayna unable to speak on his behalf and with him having no other family other than her, all of his updates and decision making were funneled through me.

I noticed that Dayna's hands had been moved to her sides. I figured one of the medical assistants had probably moved them when they bathed her. Her breathing appeared to be normal, but I knew that was just the machine working for her. I decided I had better fix her hair into two big braids to prevent any breakage. Knowing my sister, I knew she would like that. Despite everything she had been through, one of the first things she would ask after coming out of this situation was 'girl, was I looking fly'? That was my sister.

I set my phone to the newly developed FM gospel station. Appropriately so, the sounds of Jason Nelson were shifting the atmosphere, so I hummed along. I had seen on an episode of Dr. Oz that you should continue talking to patients when they are comatose because even though they were unconscious, subconsciously they could still hear you.

I grabbed each of their hands and with my head bowed, I said a prayer for my family members. I had to ask the

Lord to intercede in this situation because I needed Him to promote a break through praise. I needed all of His power to move in this place.

I pulled the recliner between the two of them and stretched out. It wasn't long before I dosed off, tired from all of the stress that comes with caring for an infirmed loved one I guess.

I'm not sure how long I had been asleep, but it was enough for my arm and hand to go numb. In my head, I thought the slight pressure that I felt was an attempt to stimulate my hand, so I wiggled my fingers a little. Again, I felt the same thing, this time with a little more vigor. When I opened my eyes, Dayna was looking over at me.

"Oh, dear God! Dayna! Dayna!" She didn't say anything. She smiled weakly and I returned the gesture. "Aw, sister. I knew He would do it. I knew He would move in this place. Thank you, God!" Tears of praise and joy moved down my face.

She tried to move her lips but was unsuccessful. The sour look on her face told me that the unpleasant taste in her mouth didn't sit too well with her.

"Let me get a nurse in here." I pushed the intercom button to summon one of the nurses on duty. Almost immediately, one of them came into the room.

"Hello! How are you, Mrs. Walters! I'm Nurse Perry." She nodded her head and made that face again. Just as I had suspected, the nurse explained, "Yes, I know your mouth is uncomfortably dry. Let me get you some ice chips, OK? Squeeze my hand if you understand what I am saying." Dayna squeezed Nurse Perry's hand and smirked.

I reached in my purse and grabbed my tube of Vaseline so that I could moisten her lips. As if unable to remember how to do so, she slowly reached up and grabbed my hand just as I was smoothing her top lip. We exchanged a look of love and thanks only sisters could understand.

She moved her head into the cup of my hand and held it there. Just then Nurse Perry came back with a cup of ice chips and a plastic spoon. After a series of routine questions, I began to feed her the chips one spoonful at a time. Being Dayna, she kept trying to help me feed her by lifting her head to each bite, but I told her to just relax and let me take care of her. And she did.

She stayed awake for two full hours. The entire time was spent with me singing to her as she listened like a toddler fighting her sleep, which eventually got the best of her.

Chapter 31 - Synatra

The place was still standing so that was a sigh of relief. One thing I was thankful for was a competent staff. As soon as I walked in, Taryn jumped for joy and ran up to me hugging my neck.

"Boss lady, it's so good to see you! Oh, my gosh! I heard about what happened. Are you OK?"

"I'm fine, Taryn, but do me favor? I don't mean to be curt, but please, let's give our undivided attention to our customers. I will update everyone on everything at the appropriate time, OK?"

"Oh, sure, boss lady. Sorry for being unprofessional, but I just couldn't help myself."

"No problem. Where is everyone?" I scanned the dining area looking at how sparkling clean the place was. The shine from the glass panels on the chandeliers revealed that they had been washed, as if the smell of the mulberry multi-purpose cleaner hadn't been my indicator.

"Well, Rosalyn was here earlier. She said she had to make a quick run and that she would be back. Adrian is in the back in the office. And that Jermaine? Well, I'll just have to let Mr. Cooper tell you about him."

"Wassup? Talk to me."

"No, boss lady. I think you'd better discuss it with Mr. Cooper."

"Uh huh. Who's this new server in here? Where he come from?" I pointed to the young man I noticed that was stopping at every table checking on our guests.

"Oh, that's Nation."

"Nation?" *What the hell?* "The man's name is Nation?"

"Yes, ma'am." She must have noticed the displeasing look I had on my face because she said, "Be easy, boss lady. I think you will find him to be an asset to the restaurant. I think you're gonna like him."

"How so?"

"Again, you'll have to talk to Mr. Cooper about that, too!" She smiled at me and returned back to the hostess stand while I trotted my happy ass to the back to talk to 'Mr. Cooper'.

Adrian was sitting in front of the computer at the main desk typing away. He was so absorbed by whatever he was working on that he didn't even bother to turn around when I walked in.

"Hey, mister. How are you?"

"Ms. Jones, I'm doing well. How are you, miss lady?" He continued to type.

"I'm good."

"Just good?" He scribbled something on the pad next to him and went back to typing.

"Yep. Just good. Take it how you want to."

He finished another word or two then turned around to face me. He was donned in a two-piece silk, black suit. The Eldridge knot in his deep, red tie gave him some mad neck respect. Not too many brothers knew about that Eldridge knot. The only reason I knew about it was because of some of our high end customers that would come in. Seeing his well-groomed, masculine, manicured hands and the sleekness of his fresh haircut made my panties moist.

"Well, that's good to hear." He stood and gave me a hug. His cologne trapped me a delicate space. I inhaled his scent as he separated from me. "I was just finishing up this week's schedule. Come on, sit down." I walked around to the guest chair – in my own office – and took a seat.

"What you all dressed up for?"

He stepped back and did a little GQ pose before answering. "Today was the day of the inspection, remember? I figured you would be with your family so Roz and I filled in for you."

"The inspection." I slapped my forehead. "Damn. I forgot."

"That's OK. We took care of everything. We passed!" He flashed me two thumbs up.

"That's what's up." I flailed my hands towards him beckoning his attention. "So, tell me about this new hire and all of these changes I've been hearing about." If he didn't know me by now I was not one to waste time or beat around the bush when it came to business.

He smirked and took his seat. Adrian filled me in on the goings on during my absence.

Seems like college-boy Jermaine didn't work out too well. Once he found out that I was going to be away from the restaurant for a little while, he started coming in later and later, if he came in at all. Seeing this change in behavior and his lack of responsibility, knowing that we had an inspection to prepare for, Adrian made an executive decision and let him go. Hell, even I had given him a warning or two shortly after he started working for me about all that coming in late. His customer service skills were on point, but he had a real disrespect for time. These young bucks nowadays just didn't believe fire burned, but I bet that ass is sizzling now.

In his place, he hired Nation, a young man he had met while he was locked up. He brought him in to replace Jermaine as a part-time server and doubled his responsibilities to include his services as our marketing specialist. This proved to be a beneficial move. He knew Nation to be a halfway decent guy that got caught up hanging with the wrong crowd. As was told to me, he would design envelopes in prison for the inmates who wanted to send something a little special to their women, wives, or mothers. One envelope in particular won him the institution's creative artist of the year award which further received national recognition by the state and then on to the governor's office. He had taken his design skills a bit further by starting his own urban greeting card line. He designed the type of cards that came straight from a homie's heart. The uniqueness of his flair aimed directly at all things from baby mommas, to dear mommas and sorry you got shot. He was very popular amongst the penile system. As it turns out, his publisher had recently signed a multimillion dollar deal with Wal-Mart. Hearing this made me wonder why a promising young man like that would work in a restaurant when he had the possibilities of the world in the palm of his hand.

He was mainly responsible for designing flyers and other literature for special promotions and events, not to mention managing our social media image. He put him on this assignment because he knew how creative a mind he had. We had gained over five thousand likes and more than three thousand followers in less than an hour. He even created a LinkedIn account for us that detailed our business practice of hiring "conditional employees" that had recently re-entered society.

Since he was assumed additional duties, he also hired another dishwasher to manage the increase in customer volume and filled the part-time prep cook position.

"So, you see, Ms. Jones. All of this was executed with Rosalyn's consent. I know she is a silent partner so I wanted to make sure she signed off on my plans before moving forward. I also didn't want you to think I was trying to take over or anything because that certainly wasn't my intent. I do hope I have your blessing on all of this."

"Well, if I wasn't going to give my blessing it's too late now." I laughed to ease the tension. "Nah, but it seems as if you have managed to set the precedence for my business and I want to thank you for a job well done." In business fashion, I reached across the desk to shake his hand and he accepted my invitation. He quickly moved this exchange to a more personal encounter by kissing the back of my hand before releasing it.

"Oh, there is just one more thing. How does Taryn fit into all of this? I didn't hear you mention anything about her."

He shook his head as he said, "Taryn is wonderful! That girl certainly knows how to woo the customers. Because of her suggestive sales technique, we almost couldn't keep up with the demand for this week's signature entrée and you know Chef likes everything to be perfect. Her marketing background definitely fits into the puzzle of this business. The girl's got talent, let me tell you!" Seeing the delight on his face told me that he enjoyed what he did, and I enjoyed having people around me that could see the vision and could help me reach my full potential for the restaurant's success. *That better be all he enjoyed doing while I was gone!*

"Good. That's what I like to hear. Well, look. I need to head back over to the hospital and check on things. I promised my sister I would come back out there to sit with her."

"OK." He walked from around the desk and assisted me to my feet, placing his arms around my waist. "Now that we're finished with the business, let's get to the pleasure!" He kissed me softly and playfully bit me on my bottom lip.

I pulled back and said, "Can I ask you something?"

"I hope so." I tapped him on the arm in response to his insult to my grammar usage.

"OK. *May*, I ask you something?"

"Sure."

"What do you think about me?"

"Uh oh."

"Uh oh, what?"

"Have you been reading one of those relationship books?" We both laughed. He tickled me on my side and I tried to wiggle from his grip.

"No, silly. I just want to know for myself."

"Definitions." He sighed and dropped his head slightly.

"Come again?" I put my hand on my hip and waited for him to *define* his meaning of definitions.

"You're seeking definitions. You, you want to define something." He took a deep breath and said, "I'll tell you what. Call me when you leave the hospital tonight and we'll talk about it over dinner. Is that good?" He sensed my slight irritation. "Before you say anything, no, I'm not stalling. Right now, I'm at work, and I just think that if we are going to have that kind of conversation it should be in a more intimate setting. And, no, I'm not talking about sex so get your mind out of the gutter!"

"Alright, alright. We'll get up later tonight then. I'll call you as soon as I leave the hospital."

"Good. I'll be waiting."

***

I hated hospitals. The hallways were gloomy, the air was cold and the odor of bed pans and bodily secretions tumbled in the pit of my stomach. Yet, here I was taking this long walk back to Dayna's room.

This time was more depressing than before. I don't know if it was the fact that I was making this journey by myself or what but I didn't like being in the same environment with "the sicklies" as I called them.

But, my situation was different.

The thought of my sister lying in that hospital bed made me emotionally uneasy. I ain't want to think about that inevitable 'what if' when it came to my sister's life. For the first time in a really long time, I realized just how much I loved my sister – both of them – and the thought of ever having to live without either one of them was a little too much for me to take in at one time. Overwhelmed with a sudden rush of fear, I paused for a moment outside of her door. I had a mind to turn around and run right back out of there, but I was here now.

The misery that met me on the outside of her door paralyzed me. As I thought about the outcome of what could be for my sister, my blood, I leaned against the wall and took a moment to relive a happier time when we were younger.

We started having our sisters' weekend getaway when I was about fifteen years old. We would choose different locations like Virginia Beach or Carowinds. One of my favorite things to do whenever we went to Carowinds was to go to the North Carolina – South Carolina border and take a group picture. It was always exciting to me to take a photo with us being in two different states at the same time.

One time we flew to Atlanta then took a connector flight to New York and back before the weekend ended. When I tell you we had a ball, I mean we had a ball.

But, I was always the one down for doing something spontaneous and out of the ordinary. So, one winter we decided to do something totally outside the box for our sister's weekend getaway.

We got a junior suite at one of the local hotels in downtown Winston-Salem. While there, we ordered some Japanese take out, ate and danced to some of the latest jams. We had our own little soul train line going with just the three of us.

Out of the blue, Dayna, of all people, got this crazy idea to go swimming. She wanted to do something to promote a bigger and better memory because she thought things between us had gotten to be a bit boring. Vay and I both thought she was playing until we looked around the suite only to discover she was gone. We grabbed our coats and hurried down the hallway towards the elevator en route to the outdoor pool area.

The sign on the gate clearly said 'closed for winter', but there Dayna was standing on the edge of the swimming pool.

"Dayna! Girl you are crazy! It's cold out here. What are you doing?" I asked through bouts of laughter.

She took her jacket off and through it on one of the lounge chairs. "Come on, y'all. This will be fun. Stop being a chicken!" She flapped her arms like the dirty bird and bwocked at us. "Let's have some fun!"

In usual fashion, Vay said, "Don't be silly! You are going to catch pneumonia if you don't come on here and stop playing."

Oftentimes it was hard to tell who was the oldest because although Vay was the middle girl, she acted like everyone's mother, including ours. Her inner strength, poise and intelligence always accompanied her by-the-book decisions. She never knew how to have *any* fun. Me, on the other hand, was too busy daring Dayna to carry on. I was a strong believer in keeping your word and doing whatever it is you say you are going to do, no matter what it is. If she was gonna play billy bad ass then I was gonna watch the show.

"No, do it! Jump in with your crazy ass!" She motioned back and forward a few times trying to psyche us out with her false attempts. I decided to up the ante a bit. "Come on. If you take off your clothes and do it, I'll jump in with you."

"For real? Don't play with me. You gonna jump with me?"

"Yeah! I'ma take my clothes off, too. Let's do it!" Off came her boots and then her jeans. She raised her sweater above her head and dropped it on the pile of clothes near her feet.

In sixteen degree weather in the prime of the new year, this fool, also known as my oldest sister, stood in her bra, panties and socks threatening to jump into the frigid waters of the hotel pool. She immersed her big toe.

"Oh, my gosh! That water is cold!"

"No shit, Sherlock!" I unzipped my coat while Dayna waited for me.

Vay walked over to one of the equipment boxes and hopped on it. 'I can't believe this' she mumbled to the sky. "Both of y'all are crazy! Y'all have completely lost your minds! What if there are sharp pieces of glass at the bottom? You know this is the off-season. What if they hadn't had a chance to clean to pool?" Vay shook her hands high above her head emphasizing the sense she was trying to talk into us. It didn't work.

"Vay, shut up, girl! You are ruining the moment!" Dayna chastised with her hand on her hip.

"Yeah, hush, before I throw you in there first," I threatened. I walked towards her like I was going to grab her and she tap-boxed the air a few times, signaling for me to remain where I was. I turned towards Dayna. "You ready?"

"No. You still have to remove your clothes!"

"Don't worry about me. You just be ready to jump by the time I count to three." I took my coat off. "OK. On the count of three?" I stepped out of my sneakers.

"OK." Dayna took her mark.

"One." She rocked back and forward. I held my t-shirt down as I removed my sweater. "Two."

"Three!" *Splash!*

That damn girl had jumped in the pool!

Vay and I gasped at the same time and began to laugh violently! None of us took notice of the other hotel occupants that had gathered on the walkway watching this whole fiasco unfold before their eyes. I could hear one of the men cheering and yelling and saying something to the effect of 'give me my damn money!' Vay was laughing so hard she hopped off the box and took off running around the edge of the pool. I was bent over, holding my stomach from the intense pangs of laughter the whole situation caused. What made me and the other onlookers almost pop a blood vessel, literally, was witnessing Vay fall into the pool after she slipped on a small puddle of water that was made from Dayna's cannonball. All of the commotion summoned more folks to open their doors and come outside.

You should have seen the way they were scurrying to find the nearest ladder to climb out of the pool. They took turns shouting and rambling 'It's cold! Oh, my Gosh! I can't believe I did that!' My tears were freezing as they poured from my eyes from laughing so hard.

Vay made it out first with Dayna close behind her. People were pointing and laughing, watching them trot from the pool area back towards the side entrance. Dayna's nipples and the fuzz from her cha-cha were promptly displayed through the white, mesh material of her matching undergarments. The sight was something to see and the men surely didn't mind watching.

Vay's fresh 'do was flopped all over her head. I don't know which was worse – watching Dayna run for cover while trying to *cover* her body or laughing at the way Vay walked in her soaking wet clothes like she had just had an incontinence accident. Either way, they both were a classic comic act and were stealing the show.

I used what little strength I had left to recover our clothes, still stumbling from laughter as I walked towards the doorway. I draped her coat over her shoulders, but not before wiping yet another round of tears from my eyes.

Watching Vay yank on the door over and over suddenly reminded me that we left the key card in the room. I yelled for one of the voyeurs to open the door and let us in the building. One of the guys wearing some maintenance-like gear removed the keys from his side and came down to meet us. He continued to laugh as he attempted to unlock the door, barely able to get the card in the lock for staring a hole into Dayna's revealing body. Vay didn't waste any time. She pushed the poor guy out of the way and ran inside. I tipped him a ten spot and closed the door behind him.

Losing myself in that moment of time, I hadn't paid attention to the door when it opened. Vay was standing there holding one of those Styrofoam water pitchers they used for patients.

"Hey, Syn. Why are you just standing out here? Come on in." She stepped aside as I walked past her. She stepped back in giving me just enough room to walk in and make my way to the chair nearest the restroom. "I was just opening the door to let a little bit of air in here."

"How is she?"

"Hanging in there. She's still not talking though. The doctors said it may be a while before she is able to speak again, but it's no cause for alarm given her condition. She was awake earlier and let me feed her." She poured two cups of water. "The nurses came in earlier to rotate her for the day and shortly after that she went back to sleep. They left about thirty minutes ago."

"And bro'?"

She paused and said, "The same," without looking at me.

Although there was nothing we could do, except to be there, I still felt like we weren't doing enough. I stood next to my sister's bed and stared at her from head to toe. She had a sense of peace and calm that covered her. The numbers and blinking lines on the stat machine, again, left me speechless and overcome with anxiety.

"Baby girl, you OK?"

The sudden question from my other sister startled me, but I answered, "Yeah, girl, I'm good" to keep her from asking any more questions. She looked at me in a scrutinizing manner. I just smiled at her and walked towards the window.

I sat in the recliner and flipped through the channels. One of those family court shows was on so I stopped there to see what foolishness the Mitchell family was talking about. It wasn't too much longer before I noticed Vay had fallen asleep, leaving me to keep everyone company. Seizing my moment, I reached over and grabbed Dayna's hand and continued to stare at the TV.

A loud, rapid beeping sound interrupted my concentration. I quickly directed my attention towards Dayna, but she was still fast asleep. Vay lifted her head, startled by the threat of what could be. That's when I realized that the noise wasn't coming from Dayna's machine. It was coming from Braylon's.

A band of doctors came rushing into the room. "Everybody out, now!" one of them shouted.

I barely got out of the chair before one of the nurse's aides came over to escort us out of the room as the sounds of the beeps quickly faded behind us.

I tried to look in through the small window in the door but it was no good. The curtain around his bed had been drawn. We walked to the waiting room, Vay weeping softly with each step. While comforting my sister was definitely a priority, I had succumbed to the eruption of my emotions. Form the depths of my soul, I reached into unchartered territory and whispered a long overdue prayer to my good God above and cried along the way.

Chapter 32 - Dayna

Six weeks later...

Finding out everything that had taken place still did not rest well with me. Jessica had taken care of the repairs at the shop with the insurance company and had held the business down all this time. She really was a great business partner. I owed her just as much of my life as I did my sisters and the rest of my family.

Learning that my husband was shot in his efforts to protect me from a lawsuit stilled my emotions. Nevaeh had stepped in – along with mom and dad – to make all of the decisions for his healthcare since I was incapacitated. Thanks to a heart-to-heart conversation she and I had a few years ago, she was able to get her hands on a copy of his living will documentation. His wish was not to be kept alive artificially for more than two weeks. Once the doctors discovered that he was eight days past his request, they needed me or a designee to approve his removal from life support. I know how hard that must have been for Vay. That act of selflessness spoke volumes as to the magnitude of love my family had for me and definitely the love they had for my husband.

Over and over I replayed the news of what happened in my mind, thus, putting me in a bad head space. Many times I would just sit in the keeping room and think. Just sit there and think, slipping in and out of consciousness.

I never thought that I would have buried my husband so soon. I thought we at least had until forever. Thoughts of my love left me unable to sleep a wink afterwards. For hours I stared at the obituary of my beloved Braylon thinking that I would never, ever find another man like him. I looked at his image remembering how he was the one who made me smile again. He was the one who convinced my heart that it was okay to love again, and now he is gone. Ever since we'd been married I have slept beside the same man, my best friend, my husband, my partner, day in and day out for the past seventeen years. But that comfort has vaporized before me and life as I knew it was no more.

What disturbed me even more was the fact that I was assaulted, more like attacked while I lay unconscious. The way Vay and Syn described it to me, one of the doctors from the hospital had come in to my room and drugged me. It was a lot to take in all at once. For the life of me, I couldn't figure out why anyone would want to harm me like that, unless it had something to do with the attack on my husband. They said I had enough drugs in my system to take out a local army in a matter of minutes and had it not been for some doctor that walked in on what was taking place, I wouldn't have made it. I later found out that that doctor was none other than Dr. Mathis, or Chance as I knew him to be. Funny thing knowing that he was the executive director of the trauma center of the number one hospital in the southeast region in the same city our family had lived in for all of our lives.

I decided I had better start getting dressed since Nevaeh was on her way to come pick me up. She thought it was best for me to get out of the house for a while and I agreed. I looked back and forth between a skirt and a top outfit and a simple maxi dress. I decided to go with the skirt and blouse since we were going over mom's house for Sunday dinner after church.

No sooner than I finished my hair, the doorbell rang. I didn't even hear anyone pull into the driveway.

"Hey, Dayna-baby. You doing alright today?"

She hadn't called me that in years. My silent answer must have given me away because she looked at me with empathy and sadness. So, I decided against being rude to my sister and coldly responded, "Hey, Nevaeh."

"Listen. We're going to meet Syn at the church and then go straight over to mom's. She cooked a big dinner, as usual." She looked over at me with a look of care and concern. "Look, I know you are still going through right now, but I do have one request. Whatever you do, try not to stare too hard at those two because if I didn't know any better, I would swear that there was something going on between them and I'm sure when we get there you will see the same. Something just doesn't make sense, you know?"

I didn't respond. Instead, I got in the passenger seat and turned to look out the window.

We drove for the next few miles or so not saying a word to one another. I listened as the words to the Sunday hymn suggested that we go to the king. I felt just like that. I felt like the only one person, the only one soul that knew my pain like a hot verse in a B.I.G. song was the Lord. Not one for wanting to seem ungrateful for the message being ministered to me in song, I began to sing along. The melody exchanged the pain I felt with the promise I know that He had for me. The tears I desperately tried to hold back suddenly began to release in a steady flow down my cheek, pooling under my chin and I left them there.

Nevaeh reached into the middle console and handed me a tissue.

We pulled into the church parking lot and parked near the east entrance. After we settled into the space, Vay overlapped her hand on mine and began to go into a word of prayer. I grabbed her hand and the two of us met in the middle and rested our heads against one another.

As soon as we calmed the spirit that was rising, we got out and made our way into the sanctuary.

The only thing I could think of was how in the world I was going to get through this. With every step I took towards the house of the Lord, I was sure that I would find my answer inside.

Chapter 33 - Synatra

It had been almost two years since I stepped foot in a house of worship, unless you want to count the time when my homegirl Jennary got married. Even then, we were only in there for about forty minutes before it was time to nae-nae all over the southview recreation center. But, this is the first time in a long time that the three of us have attended service together.

I had to agree with Vay that it was a good idea to get Dayna out of the house. She'd been locking herself in the house ever since Braylon passed. Every time you called her, she always sounded like she was on her last breath and that's if she answered the phone. The last time I saw her, she came to the door looking like death run over twice. Her hair was all over her head, her face looked sunken in and her eyes seemed distant. She was definitely not looking like the big sister I knew her to be.

After the service I caught up with the others and we engaged in a small chat in the foyer. Since Dayna and Vay rode together, I told them to go ahead of me and that I would meet them at mom's. But, from the tone of her voice I could tell that that didn't sit too well with *her*.

"Why can't you just ride with us? We're going to the same place."

Vay sounded a little irritated, so I politely told her, "'Cause I need to turn a quick corner. So, I'll see y'all when I get there, dang!" She rolled her eyes at me and took off. I hopped in my car and dialed Adrian. The phone rang a few times before he picked up.

"Yeah?" he answered loudly and in a huff.

"Now, is that any way to answer the phone, mister?" I added a bit of play in my voice to tease him a bit.

"No," he answered between heavy breaths. "It's not."

"Am I interrupting something?"

"I sort of, kind of just finished vomiting all over the bathroom."

My face screwed up at the image that popped in my head. "But, you alright though, right?" I asked with sincerity, but mainly because I really wanted him to come with me so that I could introduce him to my family as Adrian Cooper, my significant other, and not Adrian Cooper, the evening manager.

"I'm OK." He released another hard breath. "Hold on for a second, alright?"

Things between us had really picked up and after our last encounter where he told me that he had made the decision to love me if I would let him.

I was really beginning to appreciate the value of him as more than just an employee that I was sleeping with. By no means did I mean to catch feelings this strong for him, but I had and I had to admit that I liked it. It felt good to know that I finally had someone in my corner. He was the kind of gentlemen that millionaire matchmakers couldn't even pick. He had a certain swag about him that drove me crazy. No one would believe that I would end up with someone like him. Hell, I couldn't even believe it. But I have, and I wanted my family to see just how much of a difference this man had made in my life.

The screen on the dash displayed a song from some New Zealander. The beat was tight so I bopped my head up and down, waiting for him to come back to the phone. Within moments he had returnēd.

Feeling some type of way, I managed to say, "I'll understand if you don't feel like going with me." *I don't mean that.*

"No, no, baby! Of, course I want to go." Hearing the excitement in his voice turned my frown upside down. "I'm flattered that you want me to formally meet your folks. Are you sure you're OK with this?"

"Yeah, I'm ducky." He tisked at my urban vernacular. Ducky was right. I was smooth, calm and copasetic to the average eye, but I was paddling like hell underneath the surface.

I transferred the call to my Bluetooth and pulled into traffic. Well, I'm on my way to come get you. You can drive from there."

"Sounds good to me. Let me get cleaned up again. I'll be ready by the time you get here."

On my way to Adrian's place I began to get that floating feeling again. My nerves were definitely in overdrive, I thought. It's not like they didn't know him, they just didn't know him in the capacity I was planning to reintroduce him. I added more pressure to the pedal so that I could hurry and get him then we could get over to mom's 'cause a sister's stomach was about to be in her back I was so hungry.

When I pulled into the driveway he was just making his way out the house. He stopped by his car and retrieved his sunglasses and greeted me at the door. Holding my hand high above, he kissed the back of it and lifted me from the car. I hugged his neck and kissed him on the cheek. I felt so safe in his arms.

As he backed out, I noticed the tired look on his face and wondered what was going on with him. There was something he was definitely not telling me. But then again, who was I to complain or to draw suspicions because there was something I wasn't telling him either.

Each time we were together, I never felt like the timing was right. Like everything else, he would find out when I wanted him to find out and that was the end of that. As his hand rested on the gear shaft, I covered his hand with mine. The meshing of our souls chilled me as we made our way to my parent's home. And, all I did was enjoy that, too.

***

By the time we got there, dad was just pulling the ham out of the oven. The smell of the sweet and salty, fruit covered slab of swine made me gag, but I kept my composure. Nevaeh was in the kitchen buttering the cornbread muffins while mom was organizing the casserole dishes on the dining room table. Dayna was laying down on the love seat, staring at the floor.

"Hey, y'all." I walked towards mom and hugged her from behind. She obliged and reached behind to tap me on the back. "Daddy, how you doing?"

"I'm fine, baby girl. How are you?"

"I'm good." I faked a smile and looked at Vay. She looked me up and down and then directed her attention towards Adrian.

Mom removed her apron and tossed it on the back of the pantry door. "Who is this you got with you?" She leaned back and half-smiled, half-smirked at Adrian. The look on her face told me that she liked what she saw.

He was dressed in a pink button-down with white French cuffs and a pair of black dress pants. The extended-toe, hard bottoms he wore complimented his style.

"Come on in here and let's grab a seat." I pulled Adrian behind me as we made our way towards the dining room, totally ignoring mom's question. As we took our seats, and as much as I tried not to, I looked over at her. She was giving me a one of those looks that only a mother could give. You know the kind of look that started that whole cliché 'if looks could kill'.

Daddy yelled, "Alright now. Y'all come on in here and let's eat." Dayna sat upright, turned the TV off, and slowly made her way to the dining room.

We joined hands for a moment of grace over the meal that was prepared before us.

"Uhhh, let's let your guest do the honors." Daddy said, nodding his head towards me. Me and the girls looked at one another. We all knew what this was about. It was Adrian's initiation. The one thing Daddy had to make sure of was that the men in our lives, whoever they were, had some Jesus up in them and he could spot a fake from a mile away.

Hesitantly, Adrian agreed. "Shall we pray?"

He laid the law of the Lord something heavy on our hearts and minds as he went to the man on the throne. Clearly impressed, all Daddy could do was whisper 'yes' and 'thank you, Father' after every two words Adrian prayed. Even I was impressed. Mom seemed pleased with the spirit she gathered from his words, too. There was no sign that Vay or Dayna had co-signed on the experience. Both of them seemed to be in two different worlds at the same damn time.

After sitting around the table stuffing our faces, not a belly in sight was worthy of much and the 'itis' was quickly setting in. I began to rub my belly as I reclined back in the chair.

"Dang, girl!" Nevaeh, expressed. "Your stomach looks like you ate your meal and everybody else's!" She laughed.

Still leaning back, I stared across the table at her, and sarcastically said, "Nah, I'm just a little full and a little bit pregnant," I said rubbing my belly.

Pregnant? Pregnant! PREGNANT? A chorus of questions and exclamations came from every angle of the dining room. Well almost every angle. No sound came from the one seat that I expected to hear the most noise from - Adrian's.

My attention was quickly re-directed to the half-filled glass of watered-down tea that sat before me. I glanced to my left at Adrian as I took a sip. All I could see were his eyes fixed on my face and I hadn't the guts to return the favor.

Mom's face revealed that she was totally in shock and not the kind of shock a first-time, proud grandmother would have either. Her face was a bit too stagnant for me; I didn't quite know how to take that. Daddy on the other hand tried to remain calm as well, but the smile that was on his face said otherwise. He seemed ecstatic, yet taken aback by the timing of my announcement.

"Synatra, what in the world, girl?" Mom was the first one to speak up. "You know, ever since you were a little girl, you have always had this way about you, a way that negatively defines the element of surprise. Girl…" She shook her head as she pushed back away from the table and walked in the living room. The laughter from the laundry detergent commercial I could hear told me that she turned on the television which was a clear sign that she was irritated because she hardly ever watched TV.

Surprisingly, Dayna said, "Congratulations, little sister," as she got up from the table and took her plate to the kitchen. Seeing the discomfort on everyone's face made me wish I wouldn't have blurted it out the way I did, but what was I supposed to do? My name is Delanie Synatra Jones and that's just what I do. I have no filters and I have no secrets. What comes up comes out as nothing but real, raw and exclusive. Open and honest was the only way I knew to be.

The voice next to me kissed my wounded ego when the question was asked, "Baby, are you pregnant for real? I mean, are you sure?" His look of gratefulness was complemented by a sweet smile that slowly lifted the corners on Adrian's face.

"Yeah, baby. I'm sure." Finally, I turned to face him. The look in his eyes told a different story. "What's wrong? You look like you about ready to cry."

"You don't understand, love." He paused. "For the longest time, I never thought I was able to have kids. All my life I was told that it was impossible for me to procreate due to an accident I had when I was little. And, now you're carrying my seed…" He dropped his head and took a deep breath, visibly holding back his tears.

"Delayed doesn't mean denied," Vay chimed in. We were so lost in our newly found world that we both forgot she was still sitting at the table. She stood and patted him on the back and said, "Good to meet you, Adrian. Welcome to the - -"

"Oh, Lord! Come quick! Y'all get in here now!" Mom frantically screamed from the living room. Thunderous footsteps on the cedar wood floors resembled a horse stampede as we all rushed in to see what the matter was. She sat frozen solid with her butt glued to the seat and her eyes fixed on the TV screen as Daddy rested on the arm of the chair beside her. Nevaeh hugged Dayna's shoulders as they stood next to us.

The local news station was reporting that there had been a full investigation on the doctor at the area hospital that had attacked a patient. We all knew the patient to be our sister, daughter, and friend. The details that were released outed the doctor as a phony and that the perpetrator had a long criminal history.

Police say this man… The photo that was used to create his employee ID badge was boldly displayed across the screen giving me an opportunity to see his face for the very first time. Seeing his mug infuriated me. I could feel my pressure rising and steam preparing to come out of my ears.

Mom wobbled her head and began to cry out, "Oh, my baby! That no good monster hurt my baby!"

Slowly, Adrian said, "What the hell?" as he looked on in horror. He folded his arms across his chest and listened intently.

Instantly, I thought 'how sweet' he was for taking a sudden and genuine interest and being concerned for my big sisters wellbeing. I stepped closer to him and hugged his waist.

He didn't budge.

Seeing that he had called me 'baby' at the dinner table I thought it was only right that I return the flattery. "Baby, what's wrong? You look like you done seen a ghost or somethin'."

"You can say that," he said lowly as he continued to look on.

At the conclusion of the report and with one final showing of the guy's mug shot, the number to the local police department and crime stoppers was flashed across the bottom of the screen.

I noticed that Daddy never said a word. I assumed from the sweat beads that had formed across his forehead that he was hiding his anger in order to be strong for the family and especially not to ruffle mom's emotions any further.

News of the upcoming urban book club conference was told immediately following the minutes long hospital attack segment.

Mom inhaled and exhaled as she finally stood up. She stopped short of the hallway as she headed towards her bedroom. Through her own tears, she asked, "Young man, is something the matter? What's ailing you?"

All eyes were suddenly on Adrian and me.

"Ma'am, I need to tell you something." He spanned the room and considered the faces that were upon him. "I know you all are just formally meeting me, and trust me it has been a pleasure. You cooked a fine dinner, and today I have learned that I am going to be a father for the first time."

"Yeah? And?" Mom's impatience was beginning to rear its ugly head.

"Speak on it, son. What is it?" Daddy sounded. He moved closer to mom and gripped her shoulders.

"I don't know how to tell you this." He unclasped my arms from around him and stepped back. "Mr. and Mrs. Jones. Nevaeh. Dayna. Baby. The man that attacked your daughter, the man the police are looking for, the one we just saw on the news…is my brother."

Silence.

No one said a word. Daddy on the other hand stumbled as he tried to maintain his balanced. You would have thought he had seen the presence of Jesus the Christ himself with the flushed look on his face and all. With his eyes and mouth wide opened, he stared at Adrian but not for long. All of a sudden, he gurgled for air, as he clenched his chest and fell to the floor.

"Lance!" Mom screamed. "Lance, Lance, Lance! Get up, baby. Get up!"

Vay and I rushed to his side. Adrian reached in his pocket and retrieved his cell phone. "I'm calling 9-1-1, now!"

Mom began to loosen Dad's tie and undue the buttons on his shirt. It was all any of us could do to not go crazy at the thought of possibly losing our father. Seeing him gasping for air like that was too much for me to endure. The stresses boiling in my body forced the food I had just consumed back up and all over the floor. This weakened me further, leaving me heaving and gasping for what was left of the air that Daddy didn't try to get.

The paramedics arrived within ten minutes. Vay held onto me as I found comfort on her shoulder. The tears I shed soaked her blouse. Adrian kneeled by my side and picked me up to place me on the sofa. He tried to move Nevaeh back, but she was too busy trying to console mom.

We watched as the two gentlemen connected this tube and that tube while they rambled off question after question seeking information about Daddy's medical history. Mom jumped in the back of the ambulance with daddy and the emergency bus quickly sped off.

"Baby, I'm sorry! I am so sorry! Lord, what I have I done?" Adrian looked on in shame and defeat.

Through all the commotion, neither of us realized that there was someone missing from the chaotic bunch. When the news story was on about Dayna's attacker, and even with Vay right by her side, no one noticed that Dayna remained unmovable with her eyes still fixed on the television and a pool of urine puddled at her feet.

Chapter 34 - Nevaeh

Life definitely had a way of throwing you curve balls. No wonder my headaches were coming more and more frequently. I was definitely not performing at my best in the office and the quality of my work confirmed it. Folks were beginning to talk about me, mostly wondering when I was going to explode after having kept everything bottled up for so long. Weeks had gone by since I last heard from Chance. I made the decision to put off contacting him until I was able to deal with the things that had taken place. Between dealing with the traumatic experiences of my family – Dayna's attack and the death of my brother-in-law, Daddy being hospitalized after suffering a massive heart attack, and the surprising news that my baby sister was pregnant by the brother of the man that attacked our sister – I was in no mood to get to know another soul. It was all too much for me or any one person to deal with.

But, somebody had to do it.

An entire week had gone by and Dayna still wasn't answering her phone. My guess was that the way things had taken a turn she didn't want to deal with any more of life's complications.

After I got dressed, I texted Syn to let her know that I was on my way to come pick her up so that we could head out to the hospital to check on dad. She immediately responded that she was ready so I turned off the TV and headed for the garage.

As we traveled up I-85, I received a call from an unknown number. I ignored it and cleared the call screen from the dashboard.

"Sister. Something is wrong. Don't you think?" Syn twisted in the front passenger seat and sat on her leg.

I played boo-boo the fool and asked, "What do you mean?"

"Girl, think about it. Every time you call Dee she never answers the phone. You know that ain't even like her, especially if it's one of us calling," she said with arms folded.

"You're right," I agreed with her. "Let's swing by there before going to see Dad. We'll only stay for a few minutes though because Mom called and said something about we need to get there so we can all meet with the doctors concerning Dad's condition."

"A-ight. Let's just go by there, see what's up with big sis and be out," Syn spat as she now munched on a snack pack of cheese cubes and apple slices.

Moments later, we drove down the winding road towards Dayna's suburban living quarters.

"Oh my God," I said.

Nothing about the house looked out of the ordinary except for the large 'for rent' sign that stood erect in the front yard.

As we pulled into the driveway, I noticed the fresh paint sprays on the stones that edged the flower bed. I also noticed a few of the free weekly sales papers lying on the brick steps that led to the doorway. Syn didn't say a word. She just looked up at the house with her mouth wide open, even as she continued to chew her food.

I put my truck in gear and sat motionless.

Just then, a silver Infinity jeep pulled up in front of the house, stopped to retrieve something from the mailbox and seconds later parked behind me in the curve of the driveway. A middle-aged, white man tapped his phone a few times before getting out the vehicle.

We both followed suit.

He extended his hand as he walked towards us. "Hi!" He exclaimed. "You must be the Cumberlands! I sure hope I didn't keep you folks waiting on me too long."

"And just who in the hell are you?" Syn wiggled her neck in pure sister-girl fashion as she sized up the intruder. I gave her a quick glance to let her know that she needed to chill out.

"Oh, I'm sorry. Pardon my manners. I'm Jerry Partlow. We spoke on the phone earlier this week about the property, remember?"

"No, I don't remember and I don't appreciate you – "

"Synatra? Don't," I scolded. I finally reached for his hand to greet him. "Mr. Partlow, please forgive my sister. She's harmless, I promise." He nodded his head as a politeness to my explanation.

"Sure, thing. No problem." He pressed the lock button on his key fob and said, "Well, just let me get your tenant profile and I will be more than happy to show you folks around. By the way, is Mr. Cumberland planning to join us today or no?"

"No. There is no Mr. Cumberland. What exactly are you doing here and what do you mean 'you'll be more than happy to show us around?'"

Jerry Partlow, sales manager of Partlow Property Management, told us how he was contacted by one Mrs. Dayna Walters seeking to put her fully furnished property up for lease. She had made all of the necessary upgrades to the property to enhance the curb appeal and had instructed him to rent the place by any means necessary. Knowing that this area was prime real estate, he was sure that the property wouldn't be available for long as he further explained that my sister's house received more than one hundred and sixteen inquiries within the first few hours it was posted on their website. He was there to show it to a family that was relocating from Texas that gave him a ten thousand dollar deposit upfront. Seeing how he got a ten percent commission just for securing a tenant was the added bonus that put the happy in his presentation.

"I'm sorry. If you are not the Cumberlands, then who are you?" Jerry asked as if he was beginning to wonder if he had somehow violated any privacy laws by revealing too much information.

"We're her sisters. I'm Nevaeh and you've already met Synatra." Syn flicked her hand at him.

He looked back and forth between us. "I'm sorry to have to be the one to tell you this, but your sister is gone.

Yeah, she left town a few days ago, but not before leaving me with her final set of instructions on what to do about her property. Surely, she would have told her family of her intent to leave Charlotte."

"Well, she didn't." Syn said defiantly.

"Syn's right. We had no idea our sister was leaving. Did she say where she was going?"

"No. She didn't tell me anything of the sort. We only talked about the business of her house. But, if it will serve as any consolation for your troubles, I found this envelope in the mailbox underneath the keys she left for me. It's addressed to," he turned the envelope right side up and read, "'to my golden girls.'"

He handed me the envelope.

"Well, if you don't mind, I think I'll wait here a little while for my clients to arrive. It was nice meeting you two."

"Yes, but I wish I could say the same." I did an about-face and headed back to the truck.

Syn and I sat there in the truck quietly pondering more devastating news. And I began to cry. I shed a tear for every drop of heartache and agony I had stored in me. The wealth of my soul was bankrupt with sorrow and pain. Perhaps these were the dangers and the side effects of love that mother never warned me about. But, the everlasting love of the one who kept me and completed me stilled me but for a moment…and then the flood gates opened again.

Chapter 35 - Chris

Meanwhile...

Ever since I could remember, people have always treated me like I wasn't shit and had all but dismissed me as nothing more than trash from the street. And, it all started with my mom.

Her born name was Rachel Briggs, but life had me thinking her name was Dianna Cooper. I was about ten years old when I found out that Mother Di wasn't my real moms.

I was walking to the house from playing hookie from school one day. One of the neighbors got salty feelings towards her for not loaning her any money to pay her light bill and she spilled beans. She blasted all our business in the street, saying that the only reason why she had me was to receive a check from the welfare office.

Ever since then, I never had a care in the world for another female. As far as I was concerned, they could all die and go straight to hell and wait for me to get there. I was through with women. Then cowardly, I allowed the likes of some tramp to weaken me. I ended up falling for ol' girl and I regretted every moment of it since the day she left me.

When she left me, I looked for her day in and day out. I was gonna teach her ass not to mess with me and guarantee that she wouldn't mess over anybody else. Word got back to me that she moved out to LA and all I could think was 'lucky for her' until I made up in my mind to go out there and find her.

Just when ol' girl thought she had gotten away from me for good, boom, there she was front and center in *my* hospital laying in a bed that *I* was responsible for, thanks to that soft, no-good, wanna-be ass Jennis. At first, I didn't know it was her because her patient intake form had her registered only as Mrs. Walters, per the directives in her file. One could only deduce that that was her punk ass husband lying in the bed next to her as his chart listed Dayna Jones Walters as his emergency contact.

Who gave that bitch permission to get married is what I wanted to know. Had it not been for Prez's ass coming in when he did, my wish would have come true and death would have met *Mrs. Dayna Walters* in the bed where she laid. Now, I'm on the run again. But, that's alright. Payback is a bitch. You can believe that. Payback. Is. A. Bitch.

DISCUSSION QUESTIONS

1. In your family, you may be the one who always takes care of everyone else, but how do you take the time to take care of YOU?

2. Based on the background of Dayna and Braylon, do you think a love like theirs is possible in today's society especially for the nearly 70% of black women who have never been married?

3. Without giving any identifiers, how has the danger of your family's secrets, if any, impacted you? What makes you who you are today amidst those hidden truths?

4. Would you have given Adrian a second chance at making a life given his criminal history? Why do you think society is hesitant to do this?

5. The Joneses, albeit they are successful, somehow never allowed the proverbial "crabs in a barrel" mentality to overshadow their desire to help one another. How have you helped other family members or African-Americans to become successful in life? In business?

6. Why do you think Dayna left? What do you think is wrong with her?

ACKNOWLEDGEMENTS

Let me start in the only place I know how to start. I MUST acknowledge the almighty God I serve. That's not some award winning rapper's thank you either. I truly have to thank Him for planting this vision and this ability to write. This is my first novel, but I bet you this will not be my last! Thank you for making me who I am. You are the best thing that has ever happened to me!

To my parents, THANK YOU so much for being my sounding board of discipline, development, nurturing, focus, courage, love, integrity, respect and most of all LOVE. I appreciate the many lessons, the many talks – the good and the bad. Thank you for raising me to become the grown woman that I am. I can't thank you enough for all that you have done for me. I hope I have made the two of you proud.

To my aunt, Brenda, thank you for ALWAYS BEING BY MY SIDE NO MATTER WHAT!!!!!! I mean that. You have always been there to support me no matter what I do, have done or was planning to do. I really can't imagine life without you and I don't want to. Thanks for EVERYTHING!!! I love you, I love you, I love you!

I want to give a special thank you to my friend, Jayne. Thank you for listening to me as I made plans for this book. Thank you for your words of encouragement and for understanding if I didn't text you back right away! lol

Thanks, London, for your encouraging words. I appreciate the energy and the positive affirmations you provided me, whether it was an email, text message or word of prayer. Please know that I appreciate you, friend. I really do! Thanks for the photos as well! You're a star in your own right!

While I am at it, let me also thank Tony for your many words of encouragement as well and for listening to me as I envisioned the completion of this project, even if you were being your usual lame self. Nah, just kidding! ☺ You've been there since the very beginning and I thank you. Now, that's all you get!

Let me also thank one of my favorite friends of more than 20 years, Shanita, aka "White Chick" aka "Brittany". Just want to thank you for being my friend and for being a beacon of light and inspiration to me. I'll always be here if you need me. Stay encouraged! Luh ya, girl! Always, "White Chic" aka "Tiffany". *Ohhhh my gooossssssh!* lol

Thank you, Atty. Ivey L. Brown (yes, THE Honorable, your highness, Atty. Ivey L. Brown lol). Thank you for the review and feedback. I appreciate you for being there for me.

Thank you, Mrs. Nhtasasha Duncan Alston for lending me your eyes and for your help in making this vision a reality for me. I love you, Ms. Dunnnnnnncan, I mean, Mrs. Alston AKA "cuzzin'". ☺ You're the best!

I wish to thank my videographer and photographer, Terrence Williams of SayCheez Photography (www.mysaycheezphotos.com). Thank you for wowing me with your creativity! I appreciate you!

I would also like to thank Kylie Wilson of KylieWilson Illustration | Graphic Design | Presentation Layout (http://wheelson4u.webs.com). Look at what a random visit to the store can do for you! Thank you so much for your help with perfecting the cover design of my book. I look forward to doing more business with you in the future.

I would also like to honor those that have shared their words of wisdom, support, and mentoring in several personal and professional aspects of my life.

Thank you to my sista-girl mentor, Dr. Soncerey L. Montgomery, author of *The Heart of A Student: Success Principles for College Students* (www.soncerey.com). I appreciate you just for being there for a sister and modeling your grace, mercy and strength with excellence. Your kindness shown me will forever be cherished. Thank you for embracing me as you have.

Thank you, Dr. N'Krumah D. Lewis, author of *Becoming a Butterfly: From Prison to Ph.D.* (www.nkrumahlewis.com). You are one of the REALEST people I have ever met! I appreciate your story. I appreciate your grind. I appreciate your drive. I appreciate your intellect in elevating the cultured minds of today's tomorrow. Thank you for the talk and thank you for listening.

Thank you to Teddy Burris, a business associate I met in the wake of my presidency of the Staff Senate at Winston-Salem State University *(I told you what I would do when I published my first book)*. Burris is the author of *Networking for Mutual Benefit* (www.tlburris.com). I appreciate your energy and your laughter. Thank you for the networking opportunity. Keep doing what you do!

Thank you to my lovely, NaNoWriMos, Debbie Pullen and Melissa Marek. Be on the lookout for their books and other publications coming to a bookstore / ebook app / tablet / kindle near you! We sparked some magic at our first NaNo meeting. Thank you for being there and for keeping me encouraged! Rogue Writers Rule! ☺

I want to thank MY FANS!!! (That sounds kind of groovy, huh....my fans lol). Thank you for believing in me and buying my book. I hope you will continue to support me in all of my future endeavors. Please allow me to share just a few words of empowerment, if I may. Never EVER let anyone tell you that you CAN'T do something because those same people that tell you that you can't do something or try to discourage you from doing something are the same ones that are scared that you WILL do it. They can sit back like everyone else and watch what you do it!! Those people are called HATERS!! And we all know that haters make you greater, right? They make you famous, too! You may make a few mistakes here and there, but that simply means that you are at least TRYING! So, don't be afraid to be awesome! Don't be afraid to shine! See the opportunity in every opposition. Maximize every opportunity! Be courageous on purpose and have the courage to think. Live in your truth. One last thing - follow your dreams, follow your dreams, and FOLLOW YOUR DREAMS!

I would like to thank God one more time for preparing me for this journey. You said you would give me the desires of my heart and that my gifts would make room for me. How AWESOME you are! As I always do, I thank you for yesterday, today, and if it's your will, tomorrow.

Last, but certainly not least, I want to thank myself. That's right, myself! Had it not been for my love of reading and writing and for having the courage, confidence and the drive to complete something that I started I wouldn't know what to do. I am proud of myself for taking a risk, stepping out on faith and standing on NOTHING but His word for doing what I wanted to do. I know like no other person that He didn't build me this way for nothing and I plan to use everything He gave me. EVERYTHING! I know that I am destined for greatness. I also want to thank myself for living in my truth and for finally making another one of my visions under construction a reality. This is a dream come true! I bid to myself to live life so that those that know me but don't know God will come to know God because they know me. I will continue to strive for excellence and I will forever **STAY ENCOURAGED!!!!**

Thank you!

Made in the USA
Charleston, SC
03 June 2014